SOCCER SABOTAGE

A GRAPHIC GUIDE ADVENTURE

WRITTEN BY
LIAM O'DONNELL

ILLUSTRATED BY
MIKE DEAS

ORCA BOOK PUBLISHERS

For Melanie, my teammate in this beautiful game of life. And my brother Peter, who created soccer comics long before I did. Go Bromley Town FC! —LOD

Thanks to Nancy Brown for her support during the crunch times. —MD

Library and Archives Canada Cataloguing in Publication

O'Donnell, Liam, 1970-
Soccer sabotage : a graphic guide adventure / written by
Liam O'Donnell ; illustrated by Michael Deas.

ISBN 978-1-55469-163-0 (bound)

ISBN 978-1-55143-884-9 (pbk.)

I. Deas, Michael, 1982- II. Title.

PN6733.O36S62 2009   j741.5'971   C2009-900018-0

First published in the United States, 2009

Library of Congress Control Number: 2008943727

Summary: In graphic novel format, Devin and Nadia try to solve the mystery of who is sabotaging the team's chances to win the national soccer tournament. Includes soccer techniques and tips.

Disclaimer: This book is a work of fiction and is intended for entertainment purposes only. The author and/or publisher accepts no responsibility for misuse or misinterpretation of the information in this book.

Orca Book Publishers gratefully acknowledges the support for its publishing programs provided by the following agencies: the Government of Canada through the Book Publishing Industry Development Program and the Canada Council for the Arts, and the Province of British Columbia through the BC Arts Council and the Book Publishing Tax Credit.

Cover and interior artwork by Mike Deas
Cover layout by Teresa Bubela
Author photo by Melanie McBride • Illustrator photo by Ellen Ho

ORCA BOOK PUBLISHERS
PO Box 5626, STN. B
VICTORIA, BC CANADA
V8R 6S4

ORCA BOOK PUBLISHERS
PO Box 468
CUSTER, WA USA
98240-0468

www.orcabook.com
Printed and bound in China.
12 11 10 09 • 4 3 2 1

CHAPTER 1
ROARING LIONS

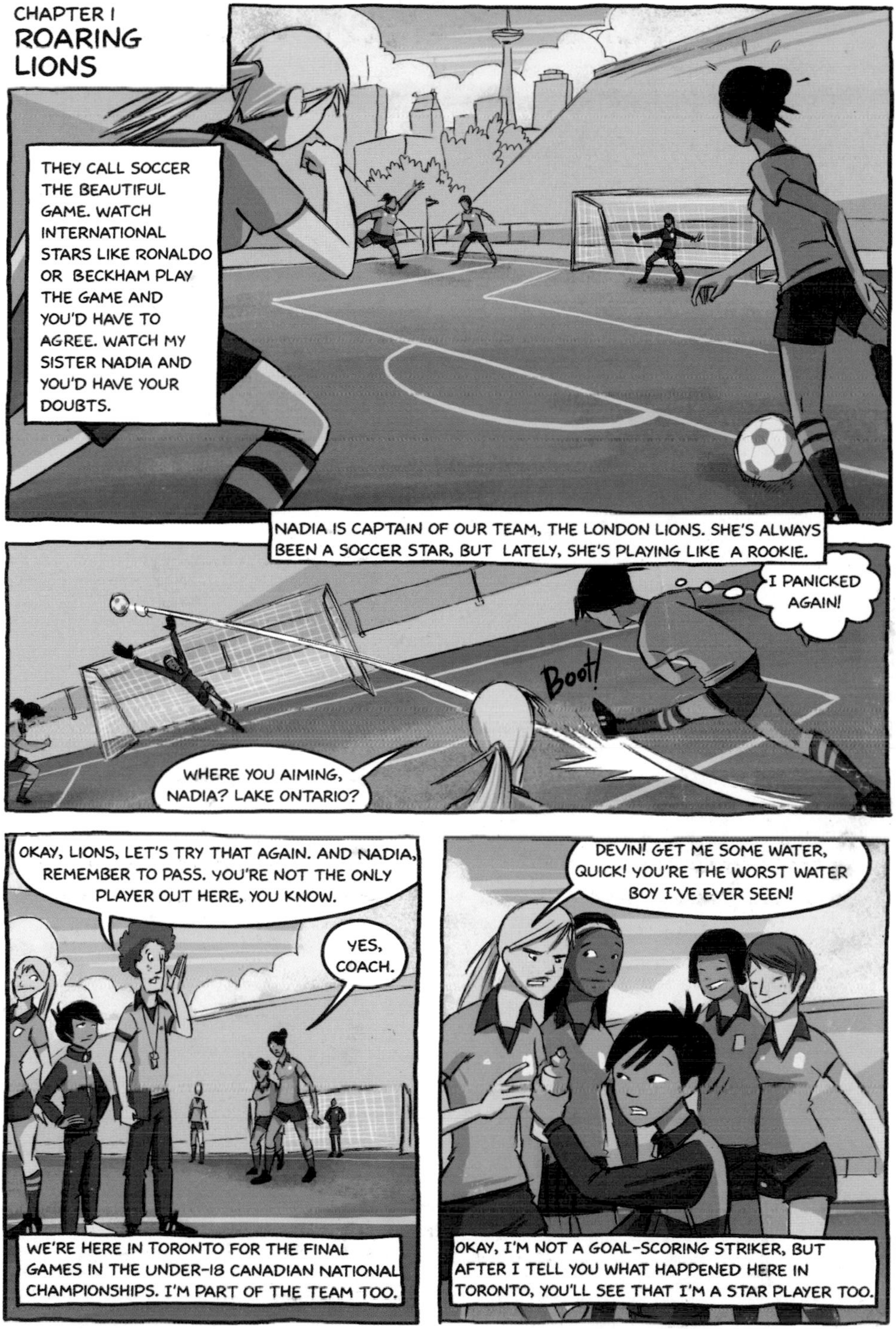
THEY CALL SOCCER THE BEAUTIFUL GAME. WATCH INTERNATIONAL STARS LIKE RONALDO OR BECKHAM PLAY THE GAME AND YOU'D HAVE TO AGREE. WATCH MY SISTER NADIA AND YOU'D HAVE YOUR DOUBTS.
NADIA IS CAPTAIN OF OUR TEAM, THE LONDON LIONS. SHE'S ALWAYS BEEN A SOCCER STAR, BUT LATELY, SHE'S PLAYING LIKE A ROOKIE.
I PANICKED AGAIN!
Boot!
WHERE YOU AIMING, NADIA? LAKE ONTARIO?
OKAY, LIONS, LET'S TRY THAT AGAIN. AND NADIA, REMEMBER TO PASS. YOU'RE NOT THE ONLY PLAYER OUT HERE, YOU KNOW.
YES, COACH.
WE'RE HERE IN TORONTO FOR THE FINAL GAMES IN THE UNDER-18 CANADIAN NATIONAL CHAMPIONSHIPS. I'M PART OF THE TEAM TOO.
DEVIN! GET ME SOME WATER, QUICK! YOU'RE THE WORST WATER BOY I'VE EVER SEEN!
OKAY, I'M NOT A GOAL-SCORING STRIKER, BUT AFTER I TELL YOU WHAT HAPPENED HERE IN TORONTO, YOU'LL SEE THAT I'M A STAR PLAYER TOO.

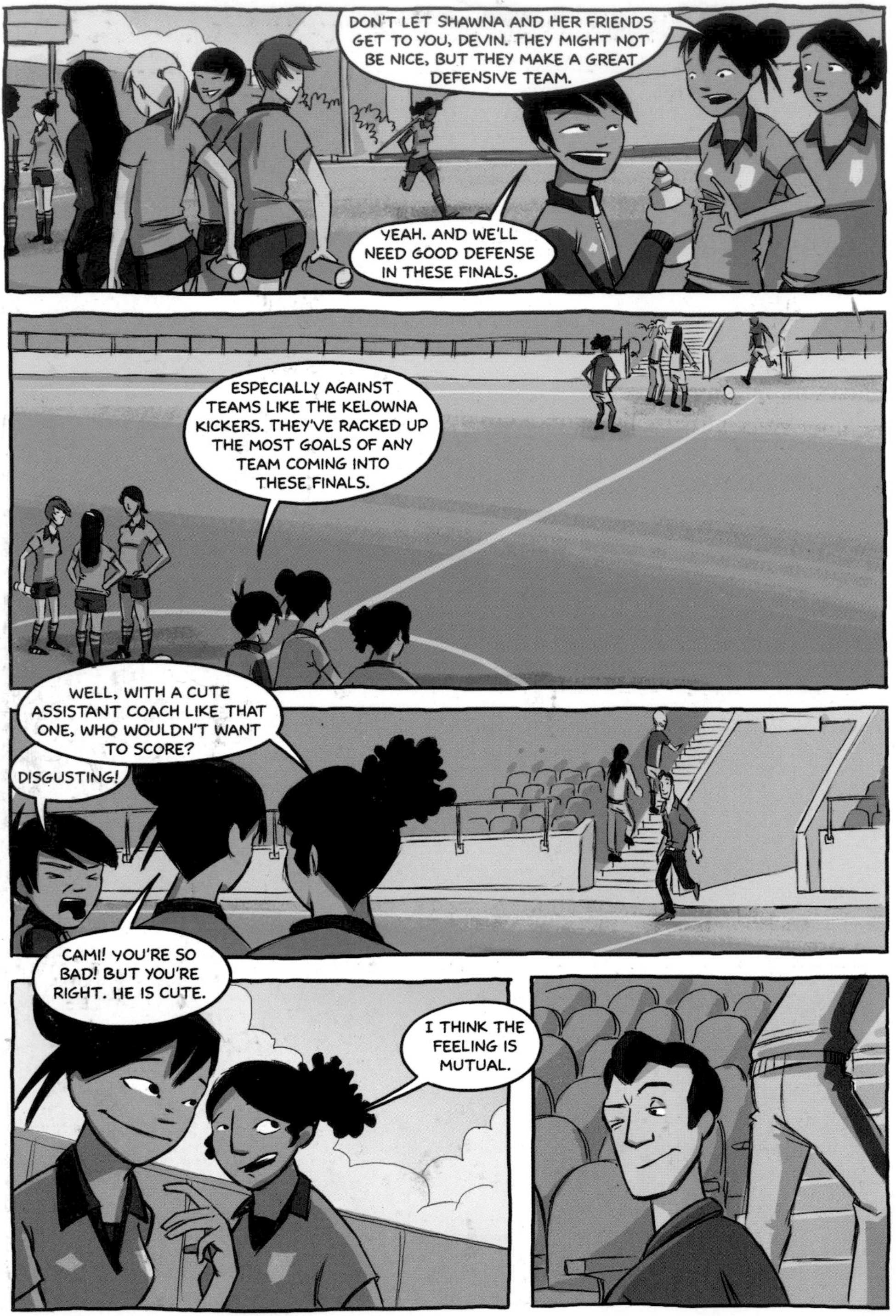
DON'T LET SHAWNA AND HER FRIENDS GET TO YOU, DEVIN. THEY MIGHT NOT BE NICE, BUT THEY MAKE A GREAT DEFENSIVE TEAM.
YEAH. AND WE'LL NEED GOOD DEFENSE IN THESE FINALS.
ESPECIALLY AGAINST TEAMS LIKE THE KELOWNA KICKERS. THEY'VE RACKED UP THE MOST GOALS OF ANY TEAM COMING INTO THESE FINALS.
WELL, WITH A CUTE ASSISTANT COACH LIKE THAT ONE, WHO WOULDN'T WANT TO SCORE?
DISGUSTING!
CAMI! YOU'RE SO BAD! BUT YOU'RE RIGHT. HE IS CUTE.
I THINK THE FEELING IS MUTUAL.

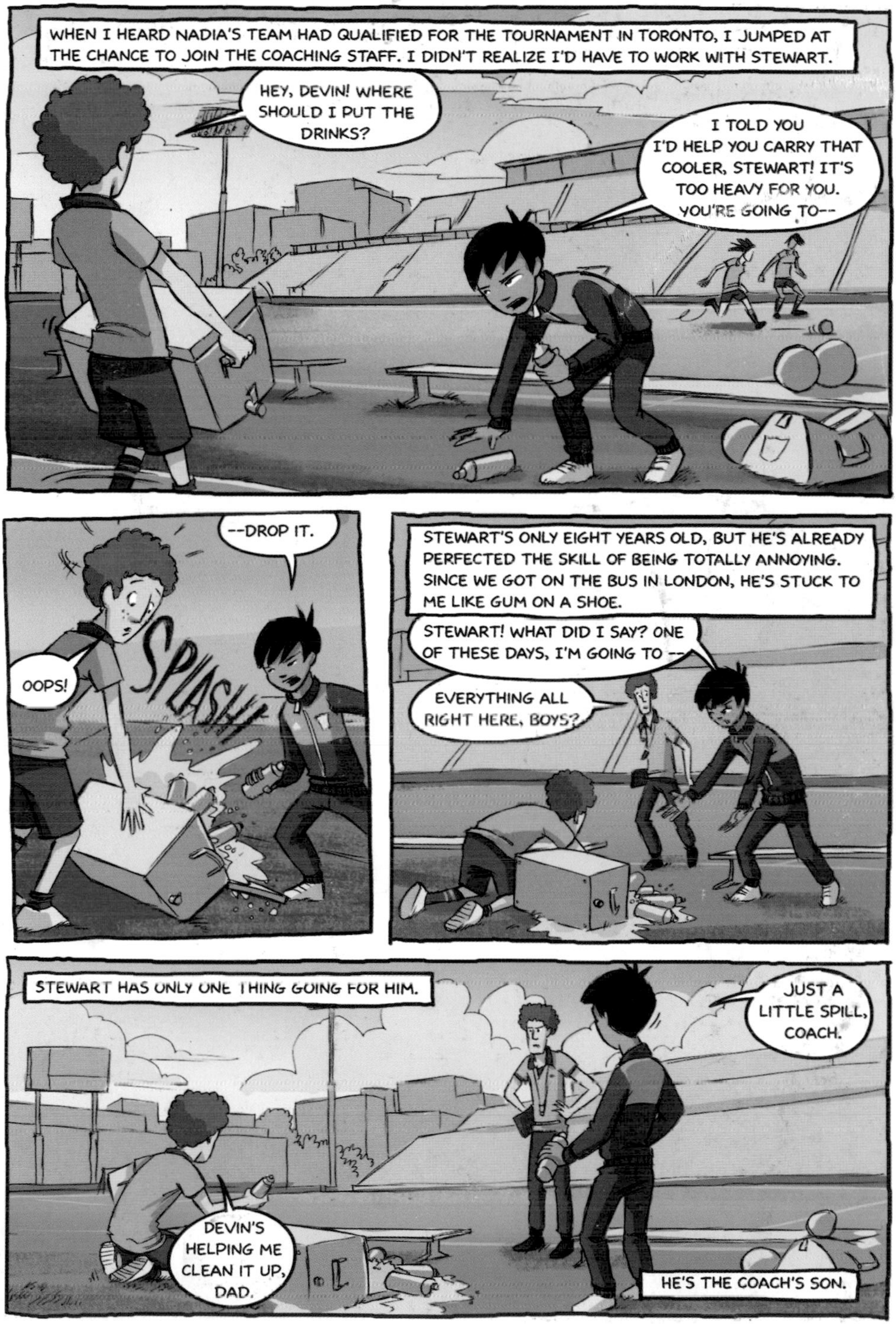
WHEN I HEARD NADIA'S TEAM HAD QUALIFIED FOR THE TOURNAMENT IN TORONTO, I JUMPED AT THE CHANCE TO JOIN THE COACHING STAFF. I DIDN'T REALIZE I'D HAVE TO WORK WITH STEWART.
HEY, DEVIN! WHERE SHOULD I PUT THE DRINKS?
I TOLD YOU I'D HELP YOU CARRY THAT COOLER, STEWART! IT'S TOO HEAVY FOR YOU. YOU'RE GOING TO--
--DROP IT.
SPLASH!
OOPS!
STEWART'S ONLY EIGHT YEARS OLD, BUT HE'S ALREADY PERFECTED THE SKILL OF BEING TOTALLY ANNOYING. SINCE WE GOT ON THE BUS IN LONDON, HE'S STUCK TO ME LIKE GUM ON A SHOE.
STEWART! WHAT DID I SAY? ONE OF THESE DAYS, I'M GOING TO --
EVERYTHING ALL RIGHT HERE, BOYS?
STEWART HAS ONLY ONE THING GOING FOR HIM.
JUST A LITTLE SPILL, COACH.
DEVIN'S HELPING ME CLEAN IT UP, DAD.
HE'S THE COACH'S SON.

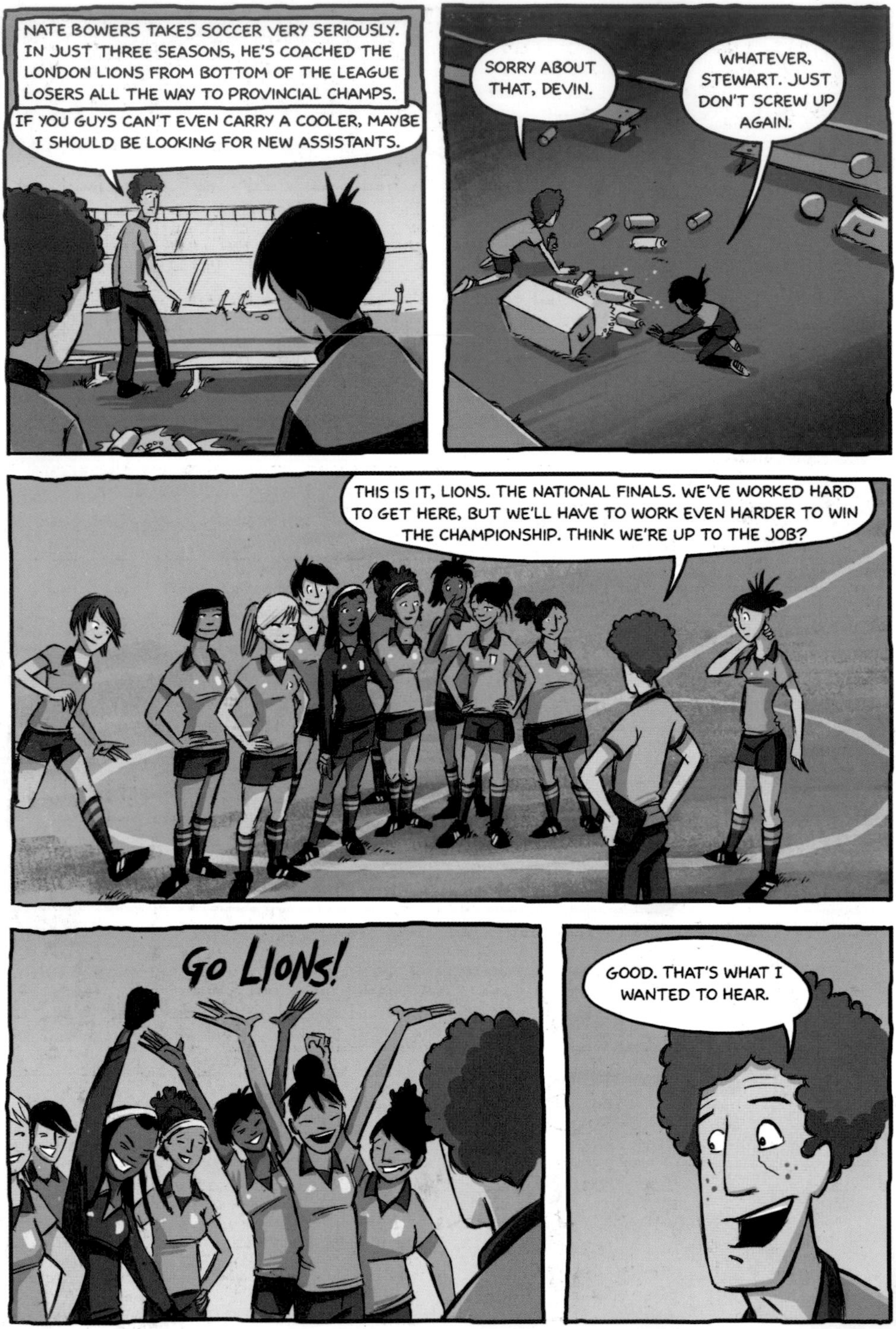
NATE BOWERS TAKES SOCCER VERY SERIOUSLY. IN JUST THREE SEASONS, HE'S COACHED THE LONDON LIONS FROM BOTTOM OF THE LEAGUE LOSERS ALL THE WAY TO PROVINCIAL CHAMPS.
IF YOU GUYS CAN'T EVEN CARRY A COOLER, MAYBE I SHOULD BE LOOKING FOR NEW ASSISTANTS.
SORRY ABOUT THAT, DEVIN.
WHATEVER, STEWART. JUST DON'T SCREW UP AGAIN.
THIS IS IT, LIONS. THE NATIONAL FINALS. WE'VE WORKED HARD TO GET HERE, BUT WE'LL HAVE TO WORK EVEN HARDER TO WIN THE CHAMPIONSHIP. THINK WE'RE UP TO THE JOB?
GO LIONS!
GOOD. THAT'S WHAT I WANTED TO HEAR.

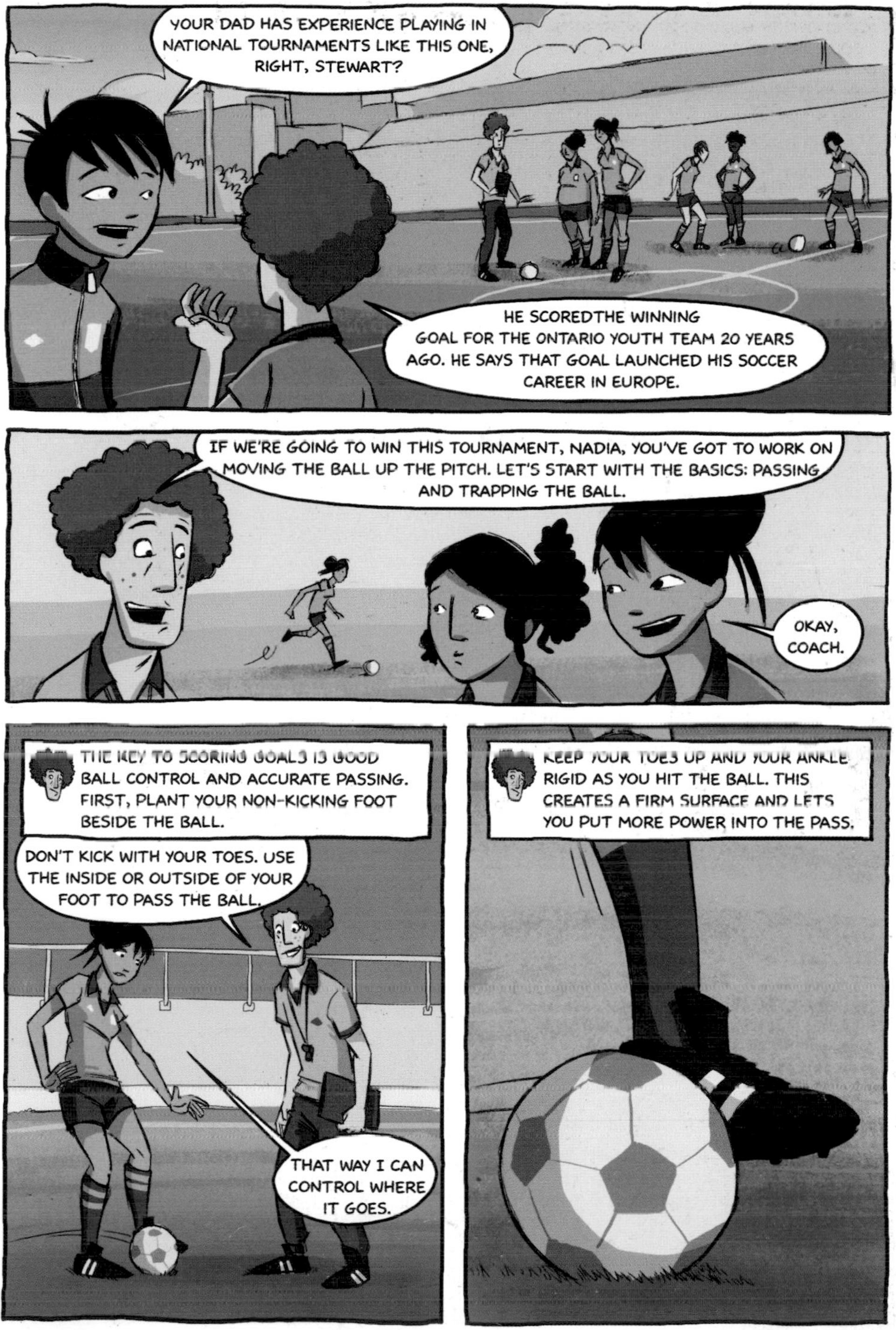
YOUR DAD HAS EXPERIENCE PLAYING IN NATIONAL TOURNAMENTS LIKE THIS ONE, RIGHT, STEWART?
HE SCOREDTHE WINNING GOAL FOR THE ONTARIO YOUTH TEAM 20 YEARS AGO. HE SAYS THAT GOAL LAUNCHED HIS SOCCER CAREER IN EUROPE.
IF WE'RE GOING TO WIN THIS TOURNAMENT, NADIA, YOU'VE GOT TO WORK ON MOVING THE BALL UP THE PITCH. LET'S START WITH THE BASICS: PASSING AND TRAPPING THE BALL.
OKAY, COACH.
THE KEY TO SCORING GOALS IS GOOD BALL CONTROL AND ACCURATE PASSING. FIRST, PLANT YOUR NON-KICKING FOOT BESIDE THE BALL.
DON'T KICK WITH YOUR TOES. USE THE INSIDE OR OUTSIDE OF YOUR FOOT TO PASS THE BALL.
THAT WAY I CAN CONTROL WHERE IT GOES.
KEEP YOUR TOES UP AND YOUR ANKLE RIGID AS YOU HIT THE BALL. THIS CREATES A FIRM SURFACE AND LETS YOU PUT MORE POWER INTO THE PASS.

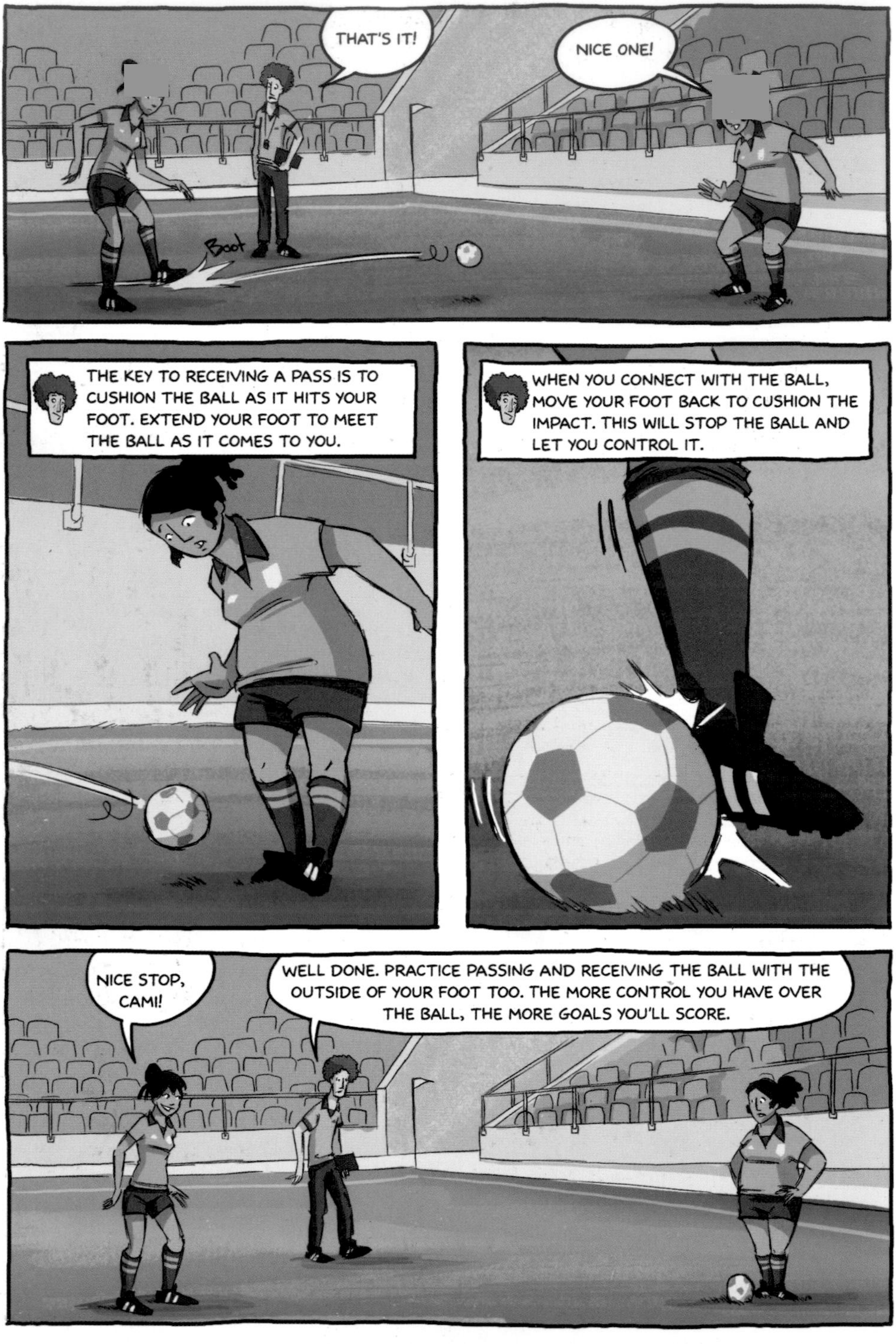
THAT'S IT!
NICE ONE!
Boot
THE KEY TO RECEIVING A PASS IS TO CUSHION THE BALL AS IT HITS YOUR FOOT. EXTEND YOUR FOOT TO MEET THE BALL AS IT COMES TO YOU.
WHEN YOU CONNECT WITH THE BALL, MOVE YOUR FOOT BACK TO CUSHION THE IMPACT. THIS WILL STOP THE BALL AND LET YOU CONTROL IT.
NICE STOP, CAMI!
WELL DONE. PRACTICE PASSING AND RECEIVING THE BALL WITH THE OUTSIDE OF YOUR FOOT TOO. THE MORE CONTROL YOU HAVE OVER THE BALL, THE MORE GOALS YOU'LL SCORE.

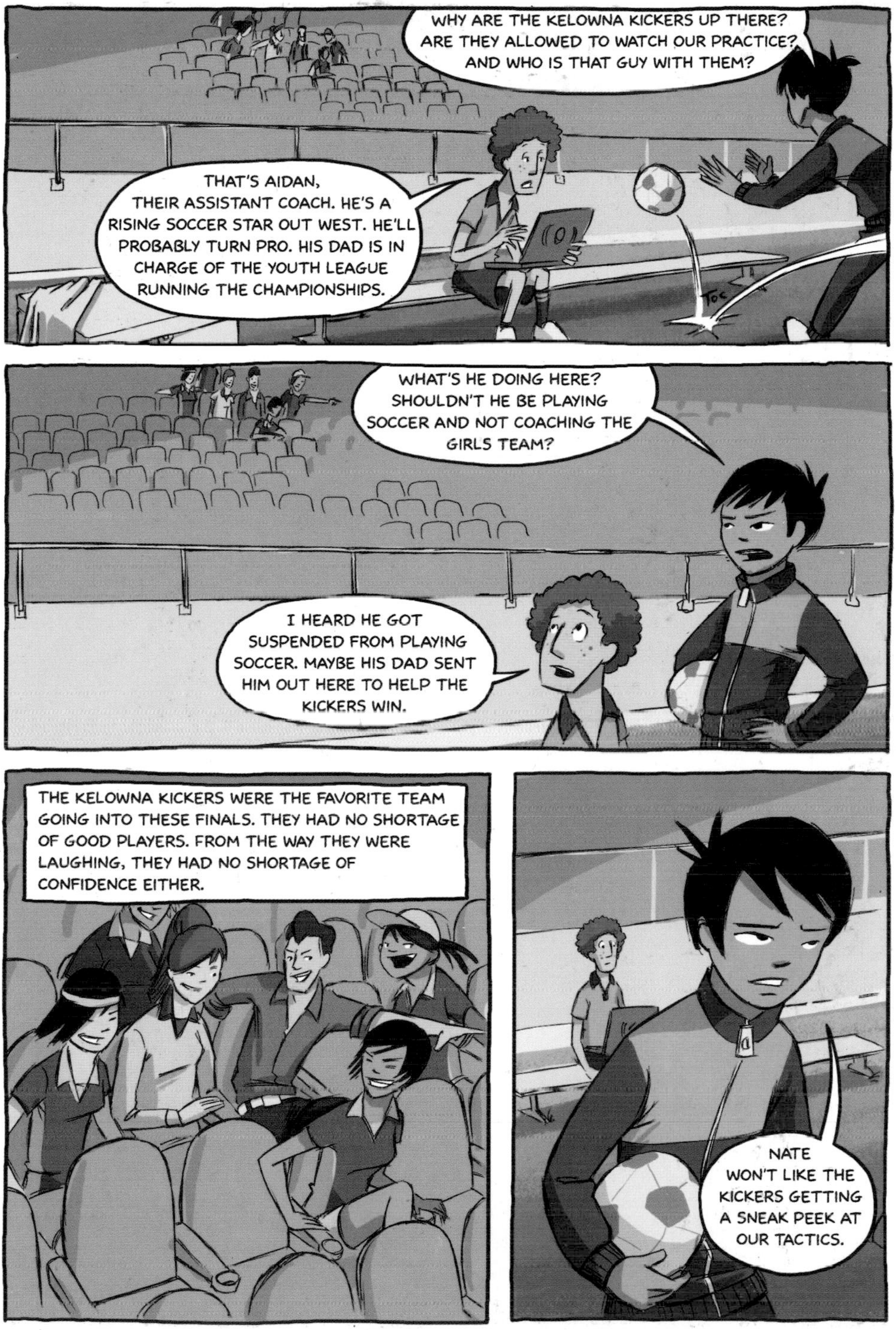
WHY ARE THE KELOWNA KICKERS UP THERE? ARE THEY ALLOWED TO WATCH OUR PRACTICE? AND WHO IS THAT GUY WITH THEM?
THAT'S AIDAN, THEIR ASSISTANT COACH. HE'S A RISING SOCCER STAR OUT WEST. HE'LL PROBABLY TURN PRO. HIS DAD IS IN CHARGE OF THE YOUTH LEAGUE RUNNING THE CHAMPIONSHIPS.
TOC
WHAT'S HE DOING HERE? SHOULDN'T HE BE PLAYING SOCCER AND NOT COACHING THE GIRLS TEAM?
I HEARD HE GOT SUSPENDED FROM PLAYING SOCCER. MAYBE HIS DAD SENT HIM OUT HERE TO HELP THE KICKERS WIN.
THE KELOWNA KICKERS WERE THE FAVORITE TEAM GOING INTO THESE FINALS. THEY HAD NO SHORTAGE OF GOOD PLAYERS. FROM THE WAY THEY WERE LAUGHING, THEY HAD NO SHORTAGE OF CONFIDENCE EITHER.
NATE WON'T LIKE THE KICKERS GETTING A SNEAK PEEK AT OUR TACTICS.

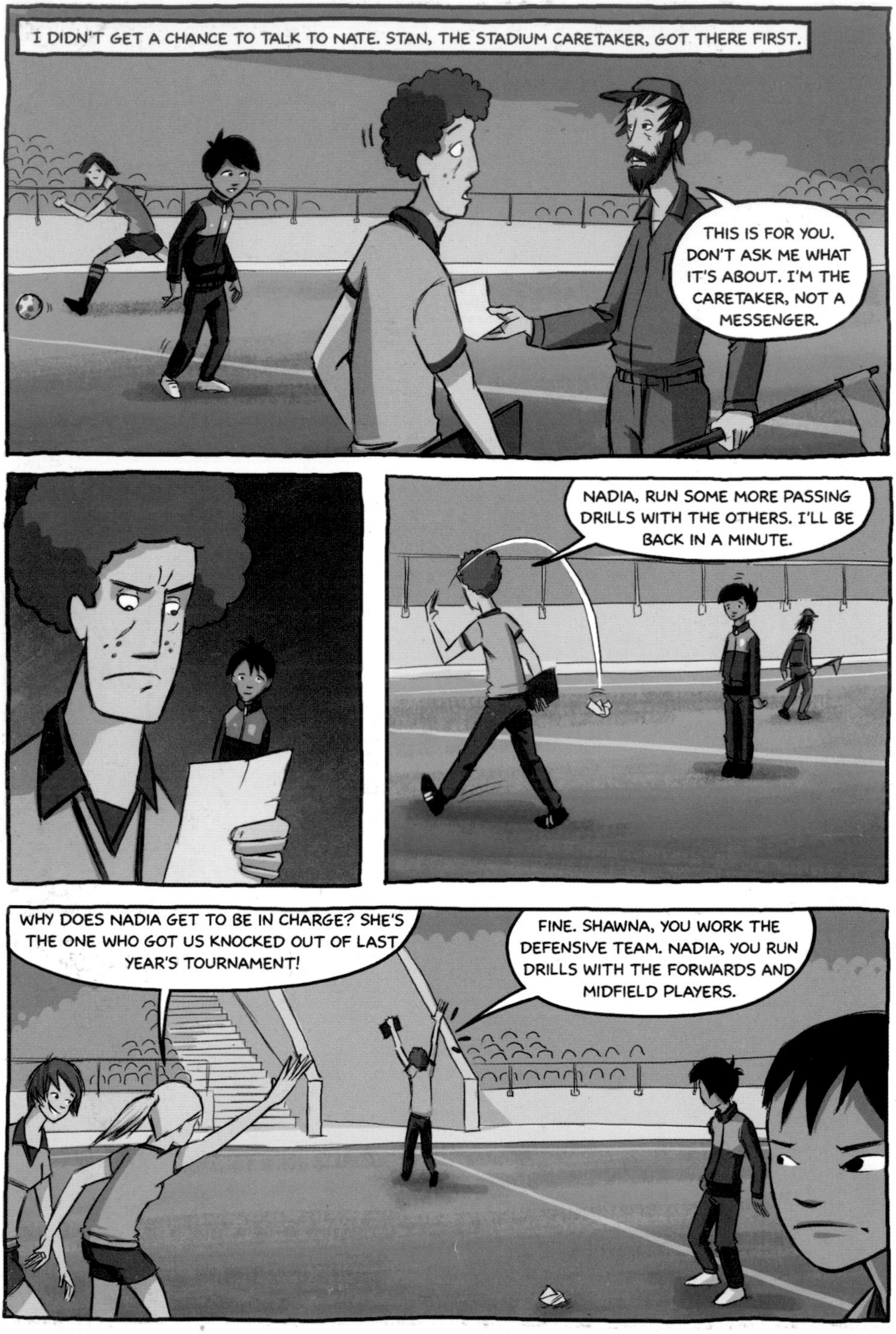
I DIDN'T GET A CHANCE TO TALK TO NATE. STAN, THE STADIUM CARETAKER, GOT THERE FIRST.
THIS IS FOR YOU. DON'T ASK ME WHAT IT'S ABOUT. I'M THE CARETAKER, NOT A MESSENGER.
NADIA, RUN SOME MORE PASSING DRILLS WITH THE OTHERS. I'LL BE BACK IN A MINUTE.
WHY DOES NADIA GET TO BE IN CHARGE? SHE'S THE ONE WHO GOT US KNOCKED OUT OF LAST YEAR'S TOURNAMENT!
FINE. SHAWNA, YOU WORK THE DEFENSIVE TEAM. NADIA, YOU RUN DRILLS WITH THE FORWARDS AND MIDFIELD PLAYERS.

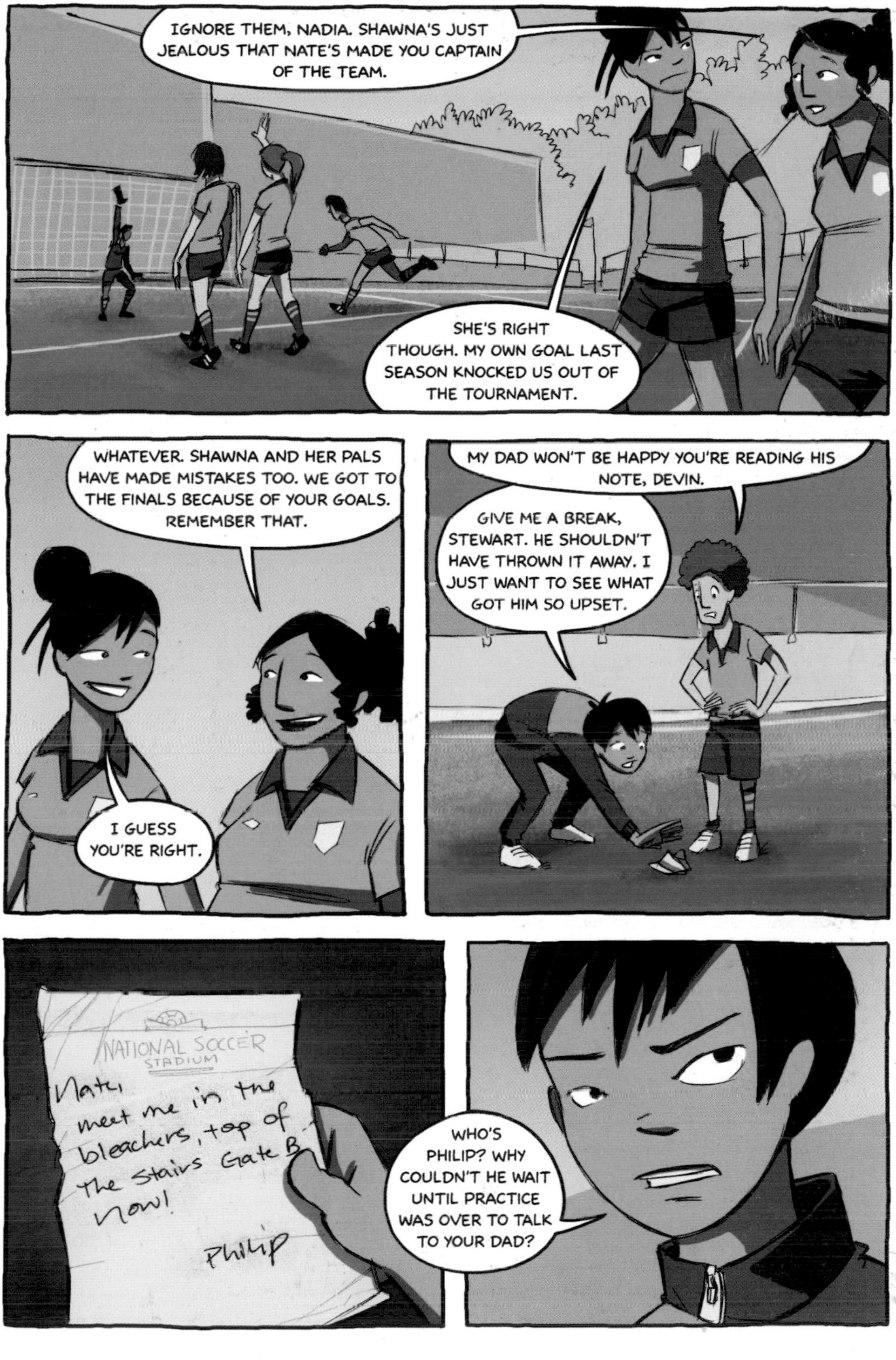
IGNORE THEM, NADIA. SHAWNA'S JUST JEALOUS THAT NATE'S MADE YOU CAPTAIN OF THE TEAM.
SHE'S RIGHT THOUGH. MY OWN GOAL LAST SEASON KNOCKED US OUT OF THE TOURNAMENT.
WHATEVER. SHAWNA AND HER PALS HAVE MADE MISTAKES TOO. WE GOT TO THE FINALS BECAUSE OF YOUR GOALS. REMEMBER THAT.
I GUESS YOU'RE RIGHT.
MY DAD WON'T BE HAPPY YOU'RE READING HIS NOTE, DEVIN.
GIVE ME A BREAK, STEWART. HE SHOULDN'T HAVE THROWN IT AWAY. I JUST WANT TO SEE WHAT GOT HIM SO UPSET.
NATIONAL SOCCER STADIUM
Nate, meet me in the bleachers, top of the Stairs Gate B now!
Philip
WHO'S PHILIP? WHY COULDN'T HE WAIT UNTIL PRACTICE WAS OVER TO TALK TO YOUR DAD?

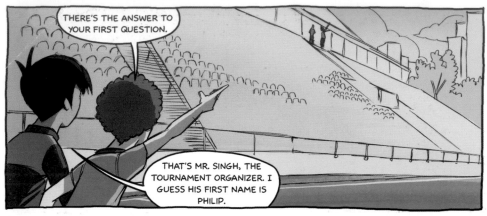

THERE'S THE ANSWER TO YOUR FIRST QUESTION.

THAT'S MR. SINGH, THE TOURNAMENT ORGANIZER. I GUESS HIS FIRST NAME IS PHILIP.

WHAT'S SO IMPORTANT THAT IT COULDN'T WAIT UNTIL PRACTICE WAS OVER?

WHO CARES? MY DAD HAS KNOWN MR. SINGH FOR YEARS. MAYBE HE JUST WANTS TO SAY HELLO.

I COULDN'T HEAR WHAT MR. SINGH WAS SAYING TO NATE, BUT IT DIDN'T LOOK LIKE THE TWO FRIENDS WERE HAPPY TO SEE EACH OTHER.

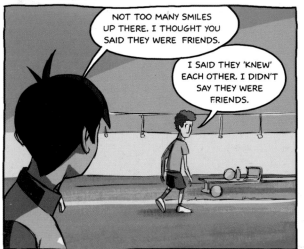

NOT TOO MANY SMILES UP THERE. I THOUGHT YOU SAID THEY WERE FRIENDS.

I SAID THEY 'KNEW' EACH OTHER. I DIDN'T SAY THEY WERE FRIENDS.

AT LEAST AIDAN ISN'T WATCHING OUR PRACTICE ANYMORE. THAT'S GOOD, I GUESS.

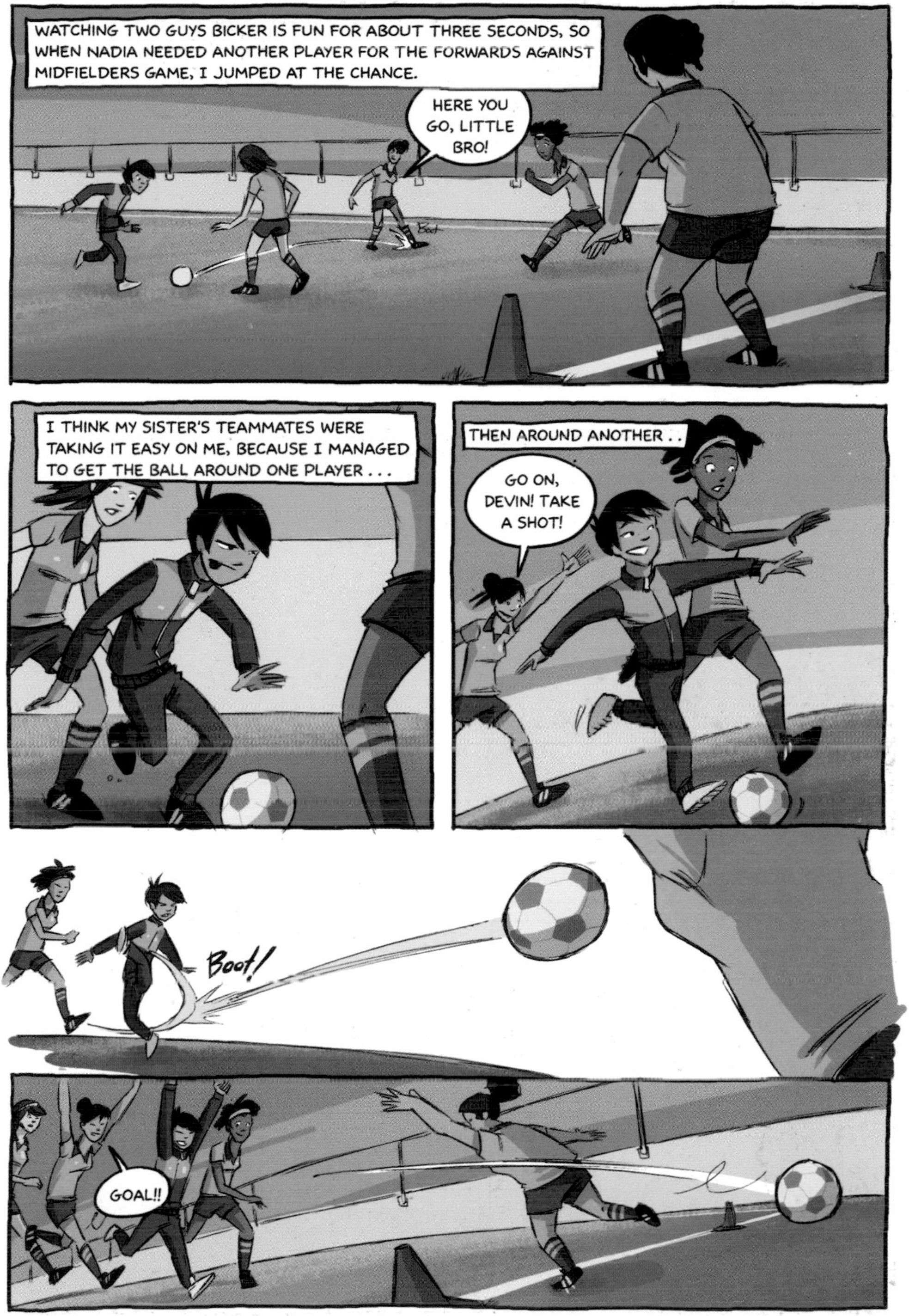
WATCHING TWO GUYS BICKER IS FUN FOR ABOUT THREE SECONDS, SO WHEN NADIA NEEDED ANOTHER PLAYER FOR THE FORWARDS AGAINST MIDFIELDERS GAME, I JUMPED AT THE CHANCE.
HERE YOU GO, LITTLE BRO!
I THINK MY SISTER'S TEAMMATES WERE TAKING IT EASY ON ME, BECAUSE I MANAGED TO GET THE BALL AROUND ONE PLAYER . . .
THEN AROUND ANOTHER . .
GO ON, DEVIN! TAKE A SHOT!
Boot!
GOAL!!

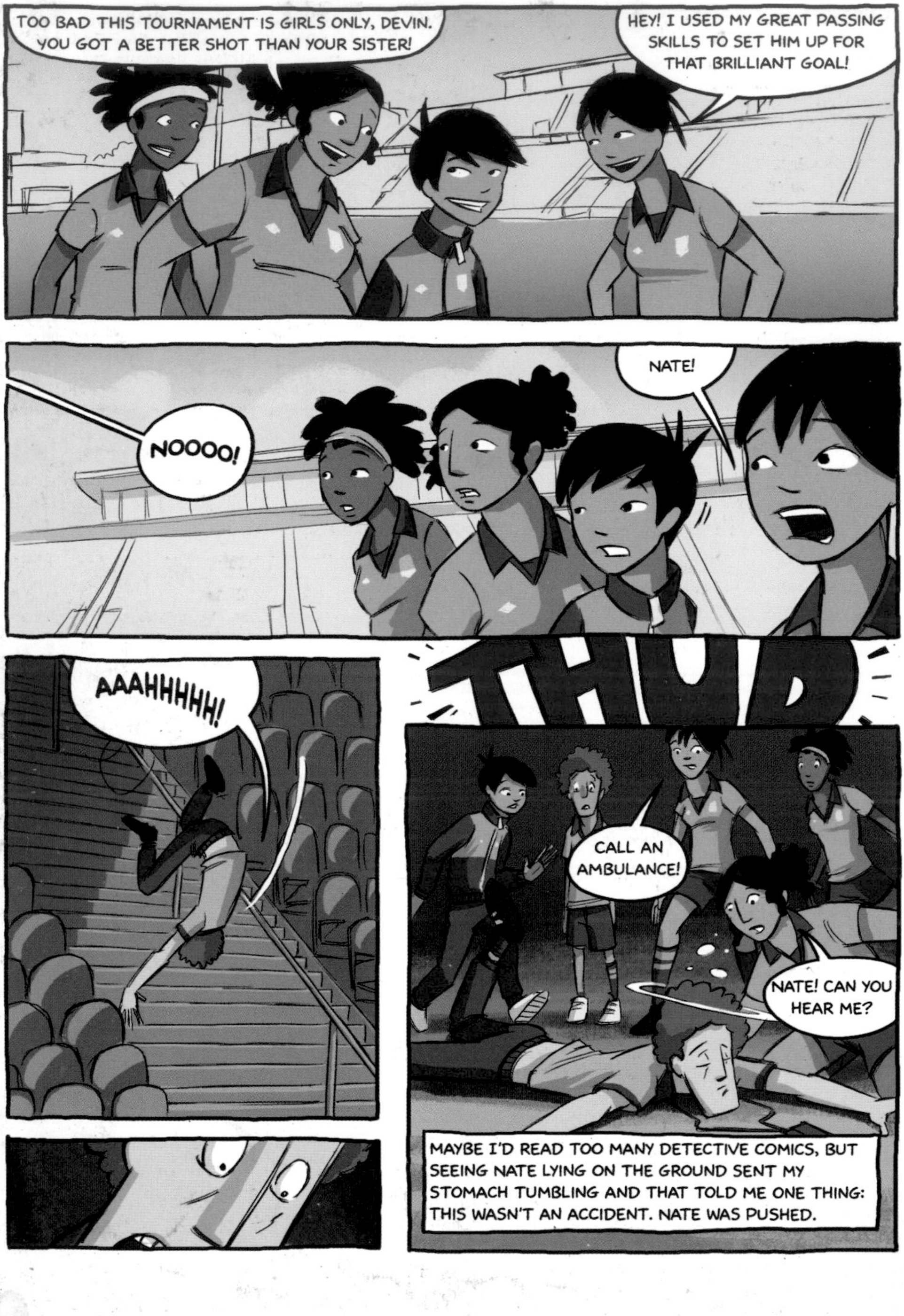
TOO BAD THIS TOURNAMENT IS GIRLS ONLY, DEVIN. YOU GOT A BETTER SHOT THAN YOUR SISTER!
HEY! I USED MY GREAT PASSING SKILLS TO SET HIM UP FOR THAT BRILLIANT GOAL!
NOOOO!
NATE!
AAAHHHHH!
THUD.
CALL AN AMBULANCE!
NATE! CAN YOU HEAR ME?
MAYBE I'D READ TOO MANY DETECTIVE COMICS, BUT SEEING NATE LYING ON THE GROUND SENT MY STOMACH TUMBLING AND THAT TOLD ME ONE THING: THIS WASN'T AN ACCIDENT. NATE WAS PUSHED.

CHAPTER 2
TOURNAMENT TENSIONS

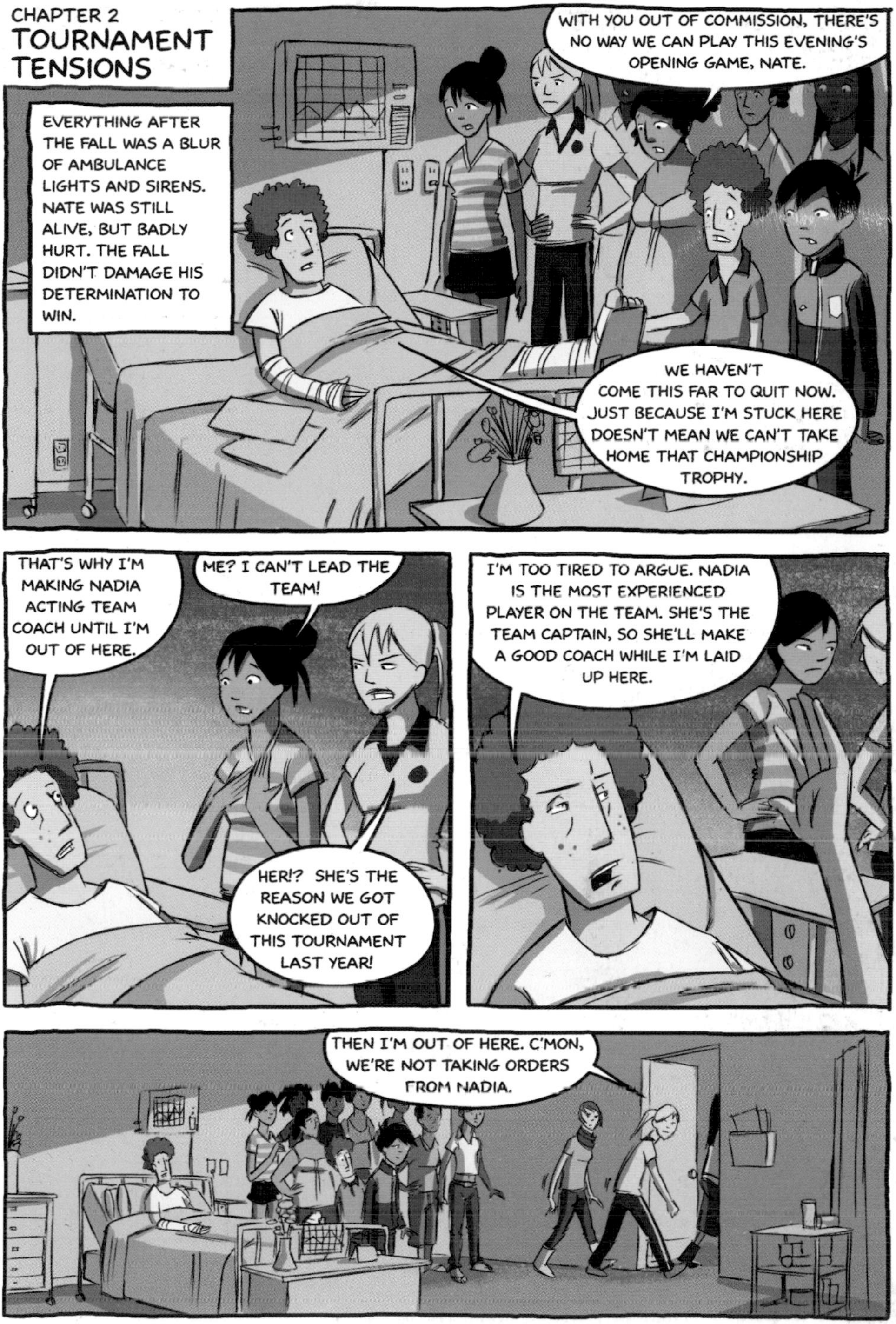
EVERYTHING AFTER THE FALL WAS A BLUR OF AMBULANCE LIGHTS AND SIRENS. NATE WAS STILL ALIVE, BUT BADLY HURT. THE FALL DIDN'T DAMAGE HIS DETERMINATION TO WIN.
WITH YOU OUT OF COMMISSION, THERE'S NO WAY WE CAN PLAY THIS EVENING'S OPENING GAME, NATE.
WE HAVEN'T COME THIS FAR TO QUIT NOW. JUST BECAUSE I'M STUCK HERE DOESN'T MEAN WE CAN'T TAKE HOME THAT CHAMPIONSHIP TROPHY.
THAT'S WHY I'M MAKING NADIA ACTING TEAM COACH UNTIL I'M OUT OF HERE.
ME? I CAN'T LEAD THE TEAM!
HER!? SHE'S THE REASON WE GOT KNOCKED OUT OF THIS TOURNAMENT LAST YEAR!
I'M TOO TIRED TO ARGUE. NADIA IS THE MOST EXPERIENCED PLAYER ON THE TEAM. SHE'S THE TEAM CAPTAIN, SO SHE'LL MAKE A GOOD COACH WHILE I'M LAID UP HERE.
THEN I'M OUT OF HERE. C'MON, WE'RE NOT TAKING ORDERS FROM NADIA.

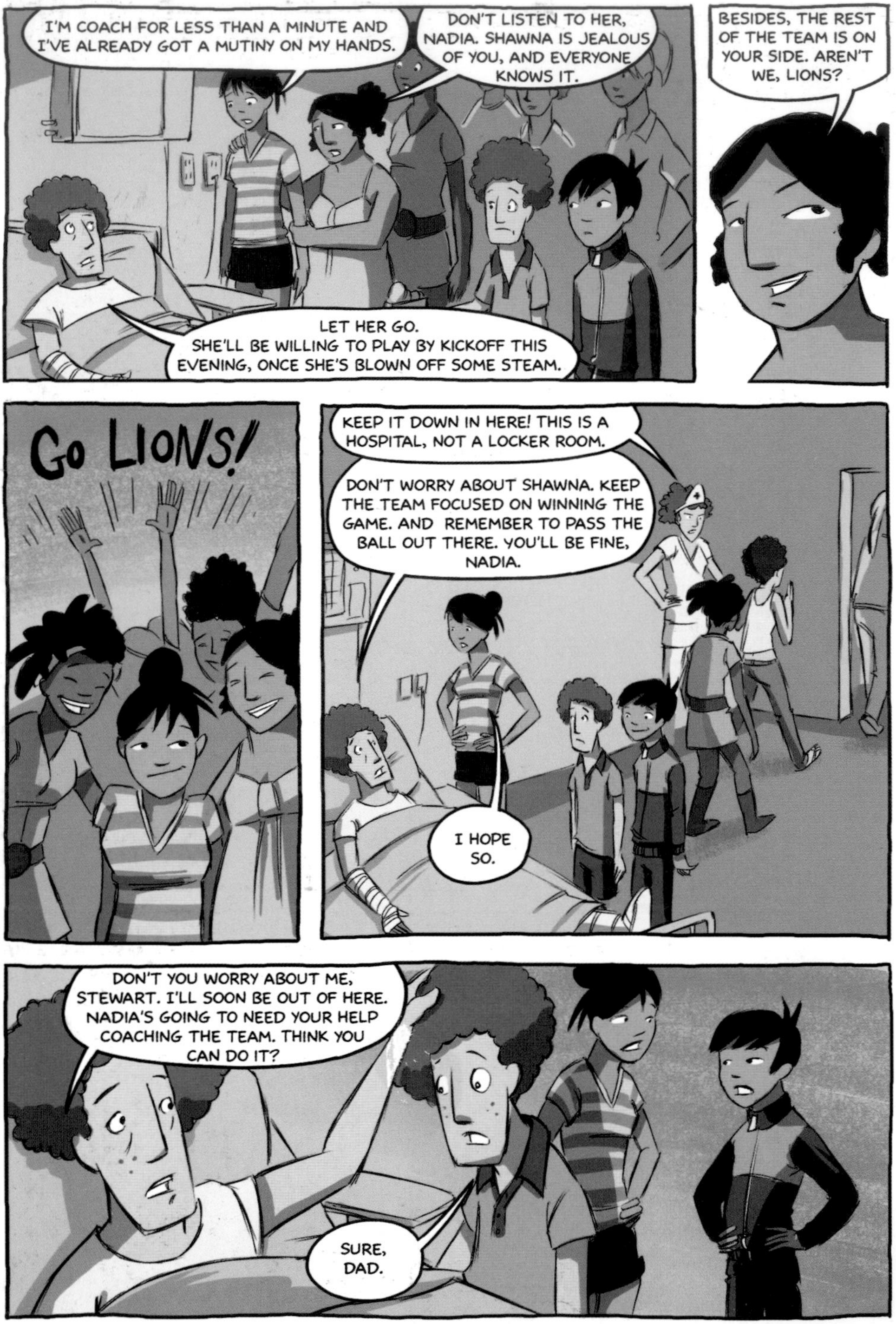
I'M COACH FOR LESS THAN A MINUTE AND I'VE ALREADY GOT A MUTINY ON MY HANDS.
DON'T LISTEN TO HER, NADIA. SHAWNA IS JEALOUS OF YOU, AND EVERYONE KNOWS IT.
LET HER GO. SHE'LL BE WILLING TO PLAY BY KICKOFF THIS EVENING, ONCE SHE'S BLOWN OFF SOME STEAM.
BESIDES, THE REST OF THE TEAM IS ON YOUR SIDE. AREN'T WE, LIONS?
GO LIONS!
KEEP IT DOWN IN HERE! THIS IS A HOSPITAL, NOT A LOCKER ROOM.
DON'T WORRY ABOUT SHAWNA. KEEP THE TEAM FOCUSED ON WINNING THE GAME. AND REMEMBER TO PASS THE BALL OUT THERE. YOU'LL BE FINE, NADIA.
I HOPE SO.
DON'T YOU WORRY ABOUT ME, STEWART. I'LL SOON BE OUT OF HERE. NADIA'S GOING TO NEED YOUR HELP COACHING THE TEAM. THINK YOU CAN DO IT?
SURE, DAD.

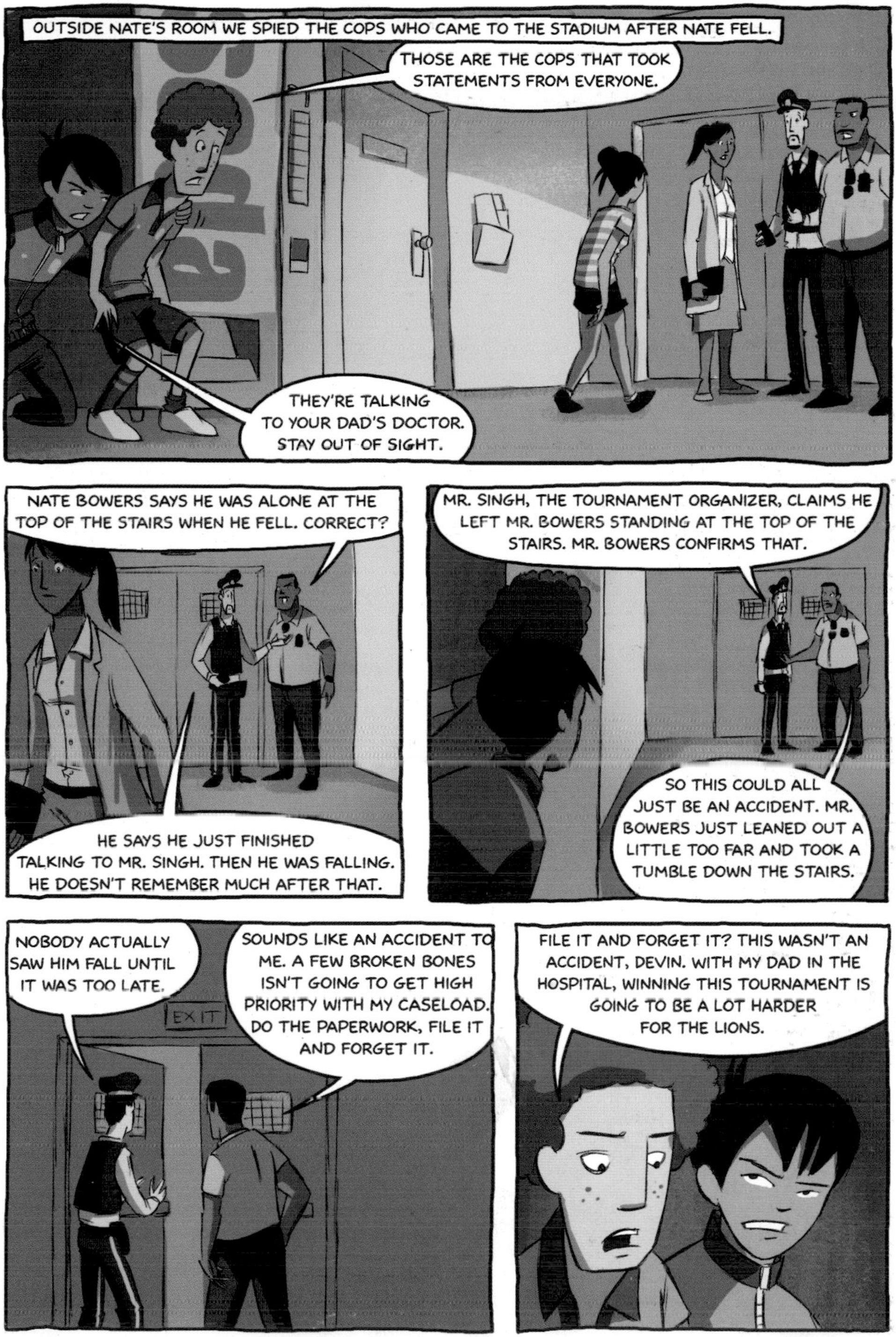
OUTSIDE NATE'S ROOM WE SPIED THE COPS WHO CAME TO THE STADIUM AFTER NATE FELL.
THOSE ARE THE COPS THAT TOOK STATEMENTS FROM EVERYONE.
THEY'RE TALKING TO YOUR DAD'S DOCTOR. STAY OUT OF SIGHT.
NATE BOWERS SAYS HE WAS ALONE AT THE TOP OF THE STAIRS WHEN HE FELL. CORRECT?
HE SAYS HE JUST FINISHED TALKING TO MR. SINGH. THEN HE WAS FALLING. HE DOESN'T REMEMBER MUCH AFTER THAT.
MR. SINGH, THE TOURNAMENT ORGANIZER, CLAIMS HE LEFT MR. BOWERS STANDING AT THE TOP OF THE STAIRS. MR. BOWERS CONFIRMS THAT.
SO THIS COULD ALL JUST BE AN ACCIDENT. MR. BOWERS JUST LEANED OUT A LITTLE TOO FAR AND TOOK A TUMBLE DOWN THE STAIRS.
NOBODY ACTUALLY SAW HIM FALL UNTIL IT WAS TOO LATE.
SOUNDS LIKE AN ACCIDENT TO ME. A FEW BROKEN BONES ISN'T GOING TO GET HIGH PRIORITY WITH MY CASELOAD. DO THE PAPERWORK, FILE IT AND FORGET IT.
EXIT
FILE IT AND FORGET IT? THIS WASN'T AN ACCIDENT, DEVIN. WITH MY DAD IN THE HOSPITAL, WINNING THIS TOURNAMENT IS GOING TO BE A LOT HARDER FOR THE LIONS.

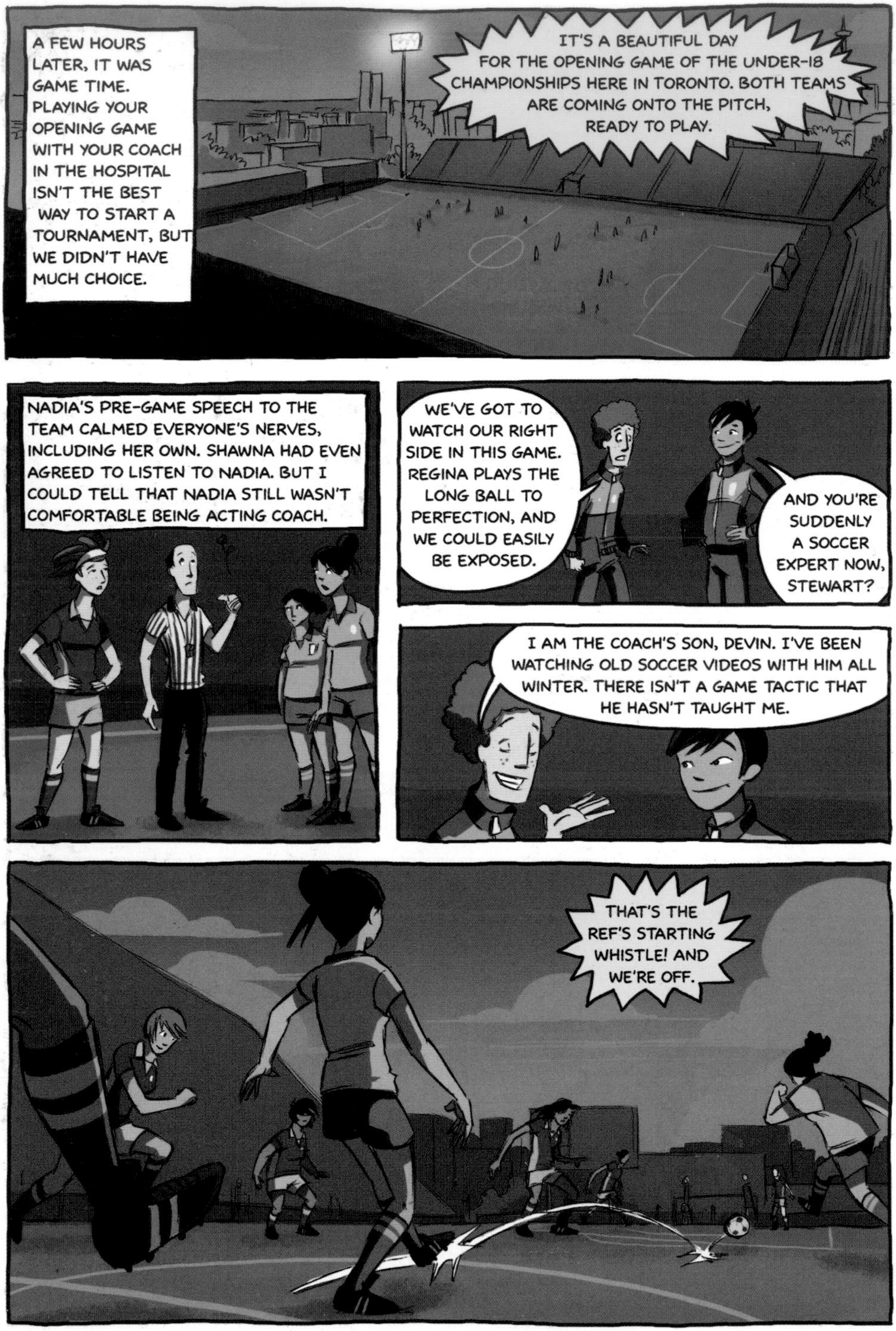
A FEW HOURS LATER, IT WAS GAME TIME. PLAYING YOUR OPENING GAME WITH YOUR COACH IN THE HOSPITAL ISN'T THE BEST WAY TO START A TOURNAMENT, BUT WE DIDN'T HAVE MUCH CHOICE.
IT'S A BEAUTIFUL DAY FOR THE OPENING GAME OF THE UNDER-18 CHAMPIONSHIPS HERE IN TORONTO. BOTH TEAMS ARE COMING ONTO THE PITCH, READY TO PLAY.
NADIA'S PRE-GAME SPEECH TO THE TEAM CALMED EVERYONE'S NERVES, INCLUDING HER OWN. SHAWNA HAD EVEN AGREED TO LISTEN TO NADIA. BUT I COULD TELL THAT NADIA STILL WASN'T COMFORTABLE BEING ACTING COACH.
WE'VE GOT TO WATCH OUR RIGHT SIDE IN THIS GAME. REGINA PLAYS THE LONG BALL TO PERFECTION, AND WE COULD EASILY BE EXPOSED.
AND YOU'RE SUDDENLY A SOCCER EXPERT NOW, STEWART?
I AM THE COACH'S SON, DEVIN. I'VE BEEN WATCHING OLD SOCCER VIDEOS WITH HIM ALL WINTER. THERE ISN'T A GAME TACTIC THAT HE HASN'T TAUGHT ME.
THAT'S THE REF'S STARTING WHISTLE! AND WE'RE OFF.

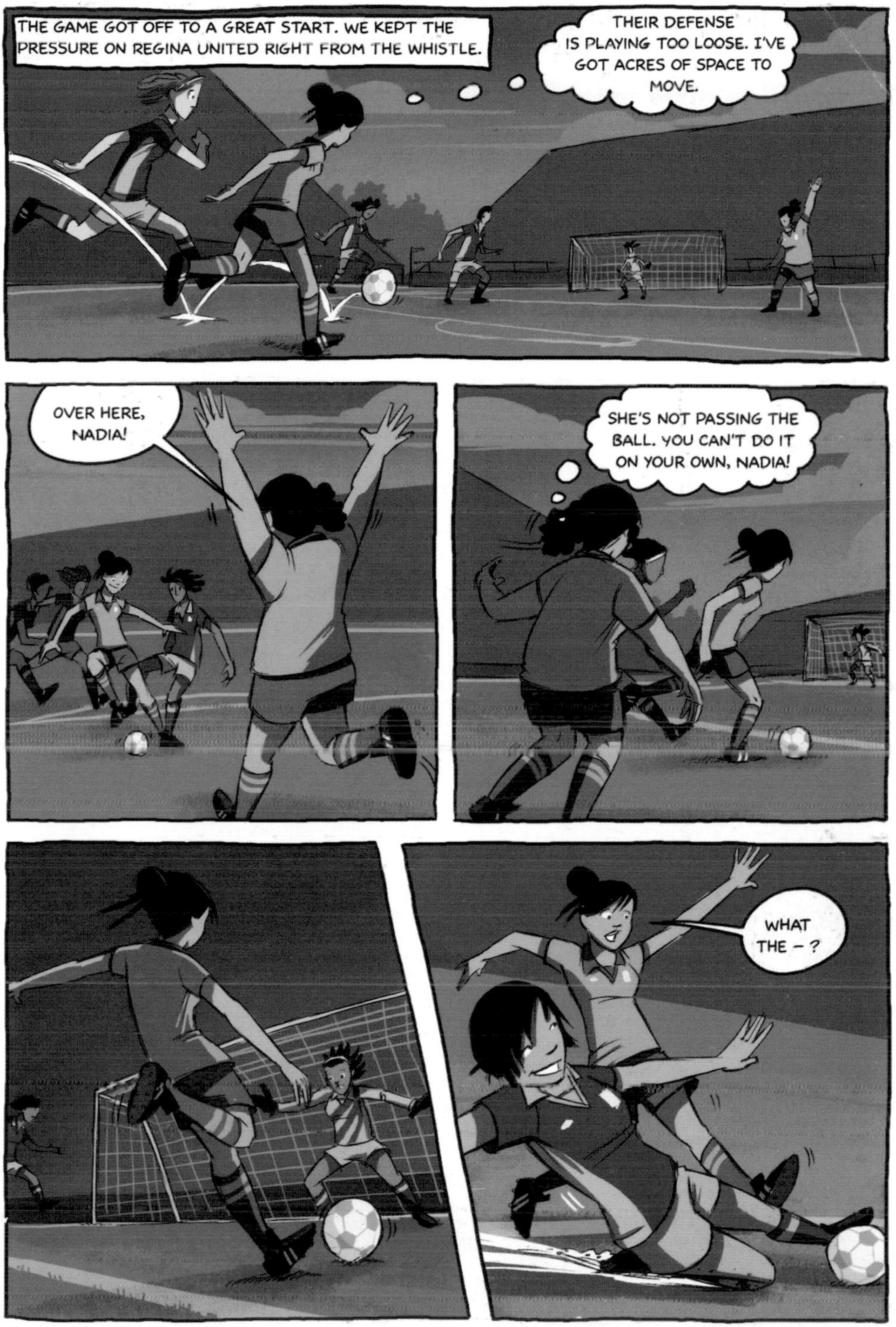
THE GAME GOT OFF TO A GREAT START. WE KEPT THE PRESSURE ON REGINA UNITED RIGHT FROM THE WHISTLE.
THEIR DEFENSE IS PLAYING TOO LOOSE. I'VE GOT ACRES OF SPACE TO MOVE.
OVER HERE, NADIA!
SHE'S NOT PASSING THE BALL. YOU CAN'T DO IT ON YOUR OWN, NADIA!
WHAT THE – ?

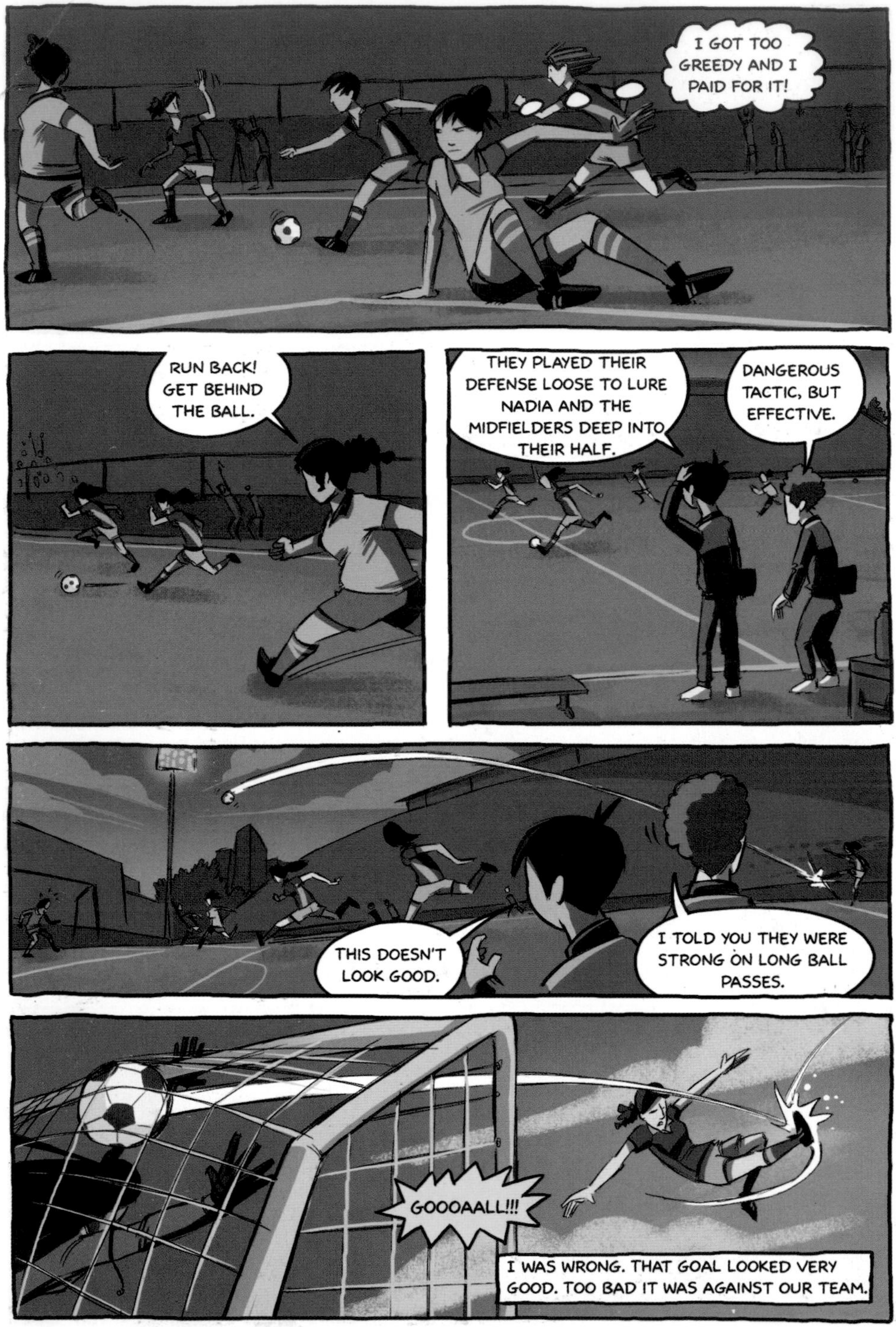
I GOT TOO GREEDY AND I PAID FOR IT!
RUN BACK! GET BEHIND THE BALL.
THEY PLAYED THEIR DEFENSE LOOSE TO LURE NADIA AND THE MIDFIELDERS DEEP INTO THEIR HALF.
DANGEROUS TACTIC, BUT EFFECTIVE.
THIS DOESN'T LOOK GOOD.
I TOLD YOU THEY WERE STRONG ON LONG BALL PASSES.
GOOOAALL!!!
I WAS WRONG. THAT GOAL LOOKED VERY GOOD. TOO BAD IT WAS AGAINST OUR TEAM.

THAT MAKES IT 1 – 0 FOR REGINA UNITED.

THANKS FOR ANOTHER SCREW UP, NADIA! IF YOU HADN'T HOGGED THE BALL UP THERE, THEY WOULDN'T HAVE SCORED!

I – I'M SORRY, SHAWNA.

DON'T BLAME HER, SHAWNA. IF YOUR DEFENSE HADN'T BEEN ASLEEP THAT PLAYER WOULD NEVER HAD GOT THROUGH.

WHATEVER. YOU'RE NOT EVEN FIT TO PLAY FOR THE LIONS, NADIA, NEVER MIND BEING OUR COACH. ONE MORE MISTAKE AND I'M GETTING NATE TO YANK YOU FROM THE TEAM!

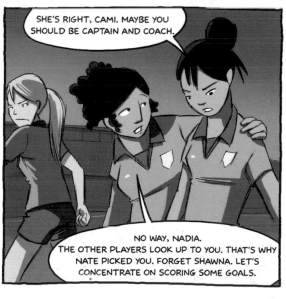

SHE'S RIGHT, CAMI. MAYBE YOU SHOULD BE CAPTAIN AND COACH.

NO WAY, NADIA. THE OTHER PLAYERS LOOK UP TO YOU. THAT'S WHY NATE PICKED YOU. FORGET SHAWNA. LET'S CONCENTRATE ON SCORING SOME GOALS.

OKAY, IF YOU THINK SO.

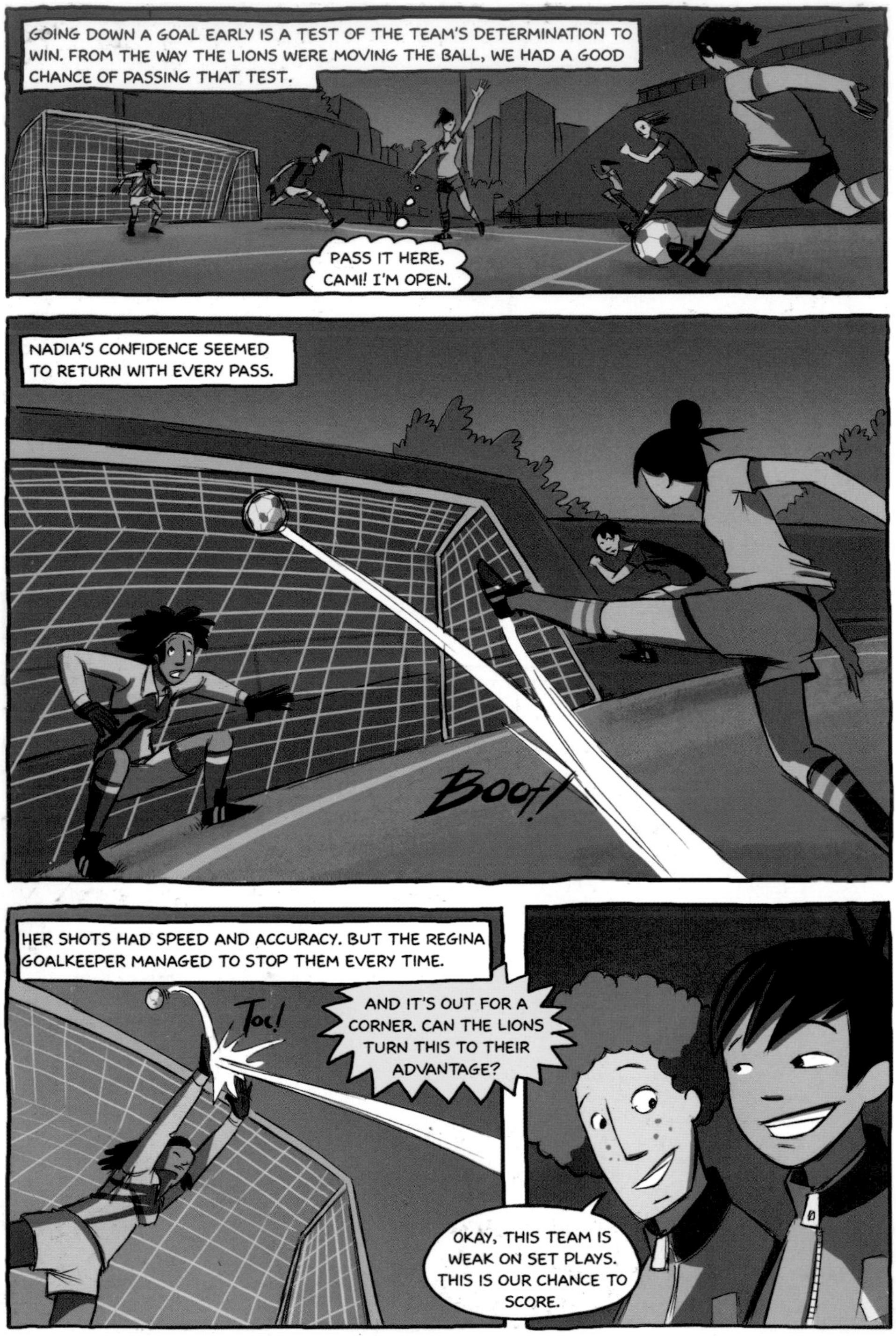
GOING DOWN A GOAL EARLY IS A TEST OF THE TEAM'S DETERMINATION TO WIN. FROM THE WAY THE LIONS WERE MOVING THE BALL, WE HAD A GOOD CHANCE OF PASSING THAT TEST.
PASS IT HERE, CAMI! I'M OPEN.
NADIA'S CONFIDENCE SEEMED TO RETURN WITH EVERY PASS.
Boot!
HER SHOTS HAD SPEED AND ACCURACY. BUT THE REGINA GOALKEEPER MANAGED TO STOP THEM EVERY TIME.
Toc!
AND IT'S OUT FOR A CORNER. CAN THE LIONS TURN THIS TO THEIR ADVANTAGE?
OKAY, THIS TEAM IS WEAK ON SET PLAYS. THIS IS OUR CHANCE TO SCORE.

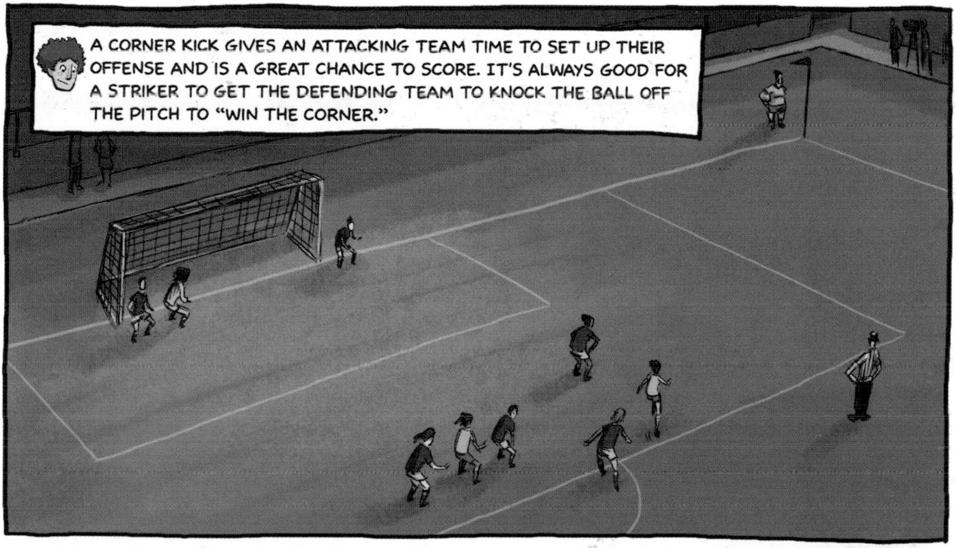
A CORNER KICK GIVES AN ATTACKING TEAM TIME TO SET UP THEIR OFFENSE AND IS A GREAT CHANCE TO SCORE. IT'S ALWAYS GOOD FOR A STRIKER TO GET THE DEFENDING TEAM TO KNOCK THE BALL OFF THE PITCH TO "WIN THE CORNER."

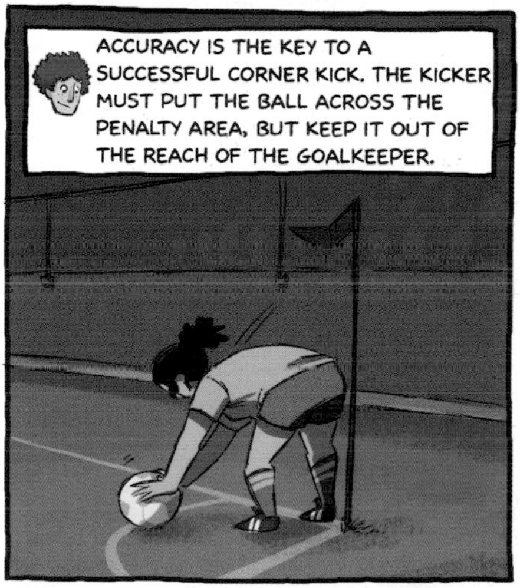
ACCURACY IS THE KEY TO A SUCCESSFUL CORNER KICK. THE KICKER MUST PUT THE BALL ACROSS THE PENALTY AREA, BUT KEEP IT OUT OF THE REACH OF THE GOALKEEPER.

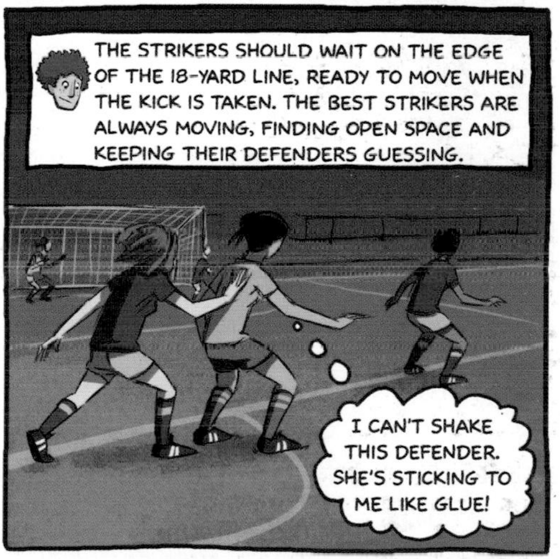
THE STRIKERS SHOULD WAIT ON THE EDGE OF THE 18-YARD LINE, READY TO MOVE WHEN THE KICK IS TAKEN. THE BEST STRIKERS ARE ALWAYS MOVING, FINDING OPEN SPACE AND KEEPING THEIR DEFENDERS GUESSING.
I CAN'T SHAKE THIS DEFENDER. SHE'S STICKING TO ME LIKE GLUE!

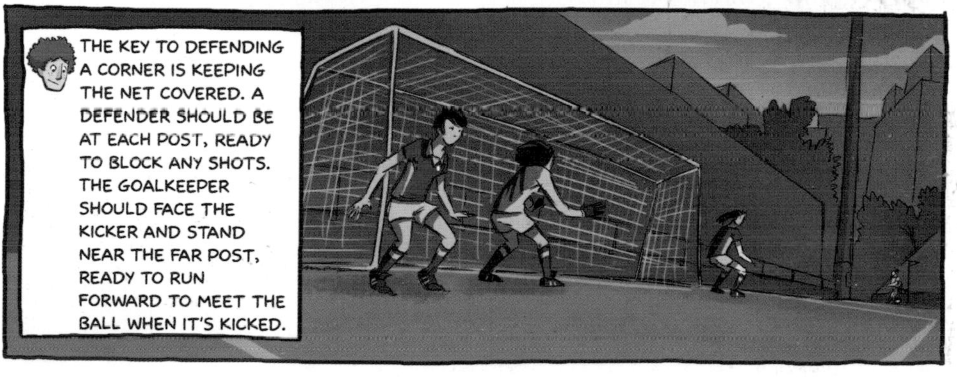
THE KEY TO DEFENDING A CORNER IS KEEPING THE NET COVERED. A DEFENDER SHOULD BE AT EACH POST, READY TO BLOCK ANY SHOTS. THE GOALKEEPER SHOULD FACE THE KICKER AND STAND NEAR THE FAR POST, READY TO RUN FORWARD TO MEET THE BALL WHEN IT'S KICKED.

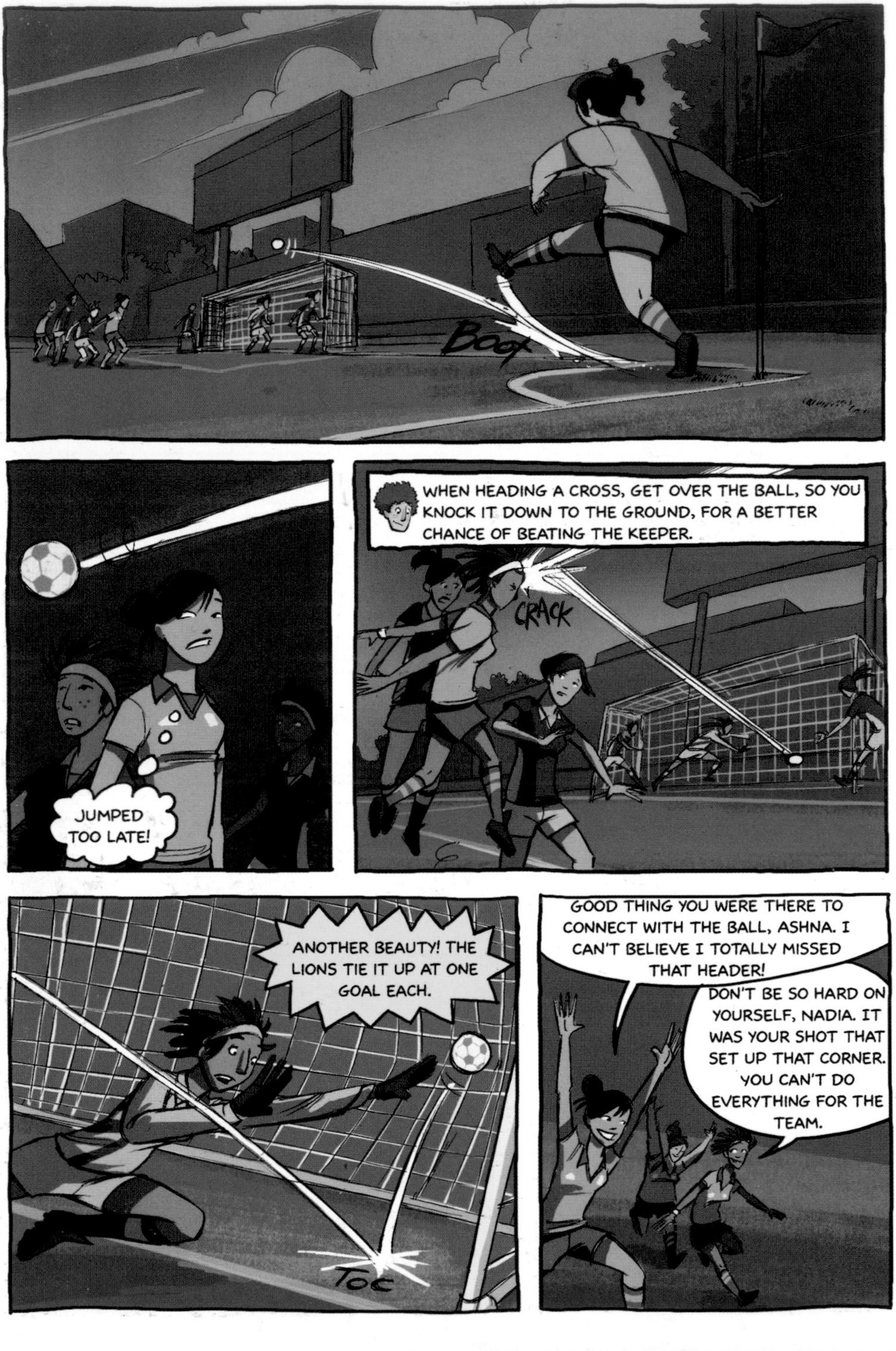
BOOT
WHEN HEADING A CROSS, GET OVER THE BALL, SO YOU KNOCK IT DOWN TO THE GROUND, FOR A BETTER CHANCE OF BEATING THE KEEPER.
JUMPED TOO LATE!
CRACK
ANOTHER BEAUTY! THE LIONS TIE IT UP AT ONE GOAL EACH.
TOC
GOOD THING YOU WERE THERE TO CONNECT WITH THE BALL, ASHNA. I CAN'T BELIEVE I TOTALLY MISSED THAT HEADER!
DON'T BE SO HARD ON YOURSELF, NADIA. IT WAS YOUR SHOT THAT SET UP THAT CORNER. YOU CAN'T DO EVERYTHING FOR THE TEAM.

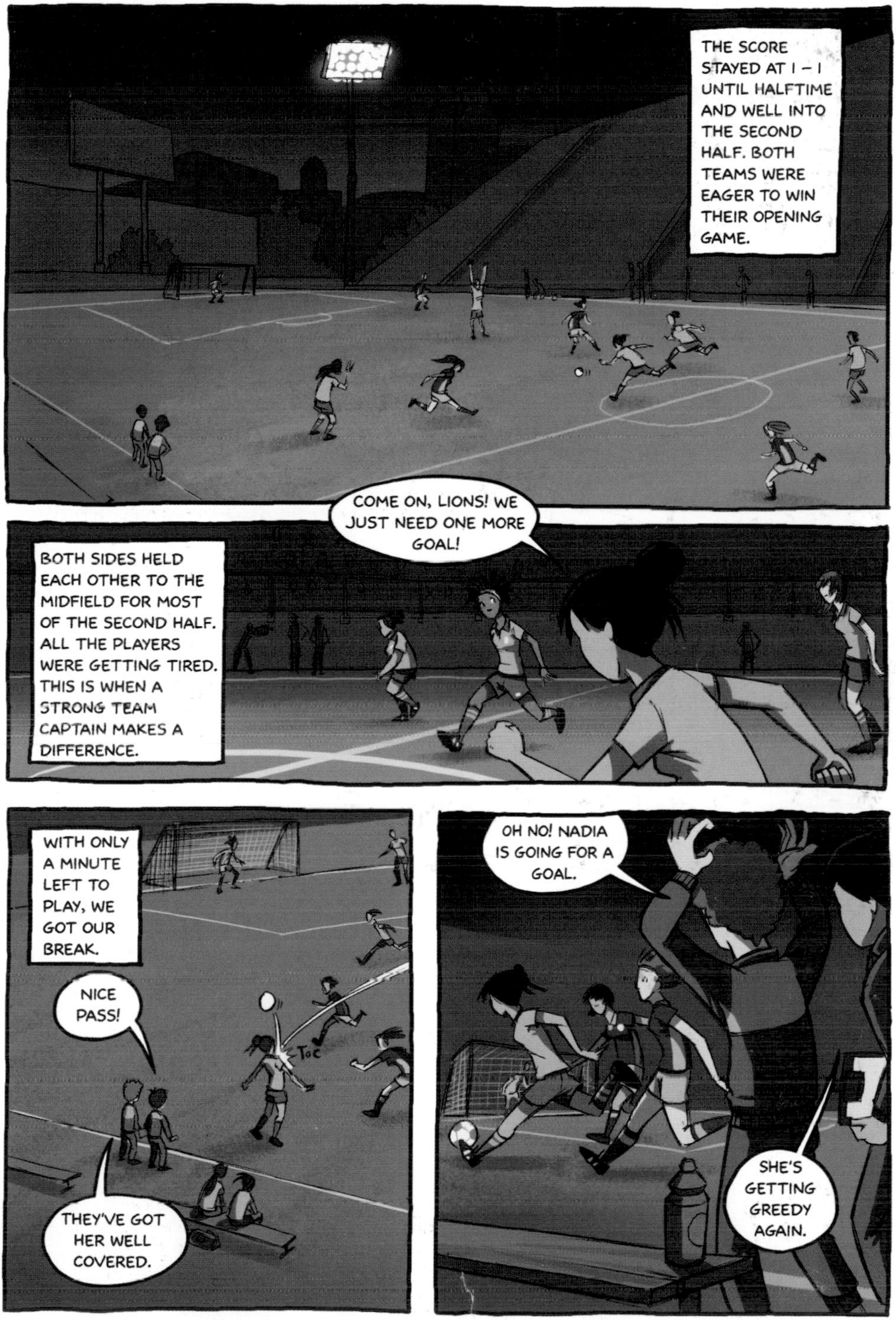
THE SCORE STAYED AT 1 – 1 UNTIL HALFTIME AND WELL INTO THE SECOND HALF. BOTH TEAMS WERE EAGER TO WIN THEIR OPENING GAME.
BOTH SIDES HELD EACH OTHER TO THE MIDFIELD FOR MOST OF THE SECOND HALF. ALL THE PLAYERS WERE GETTING TIRED. THIS IS WHEN A STRONG TEAM CAPTAIN MAKES A DIFFERENCE.
COME ON, LIONS! WE JUST NEED ONE MORE GOAL!
WITH ONLY A MINUTE LEFT TO PLAY, WE GOT OUR BREAK.
NICE PASS!
TOC
THEY'VE GOT HER WELL COVERED.
OH NO! NADIA IS GOING FOR A GOAL.
SHE'S GETTING GREEDY AGAIN.

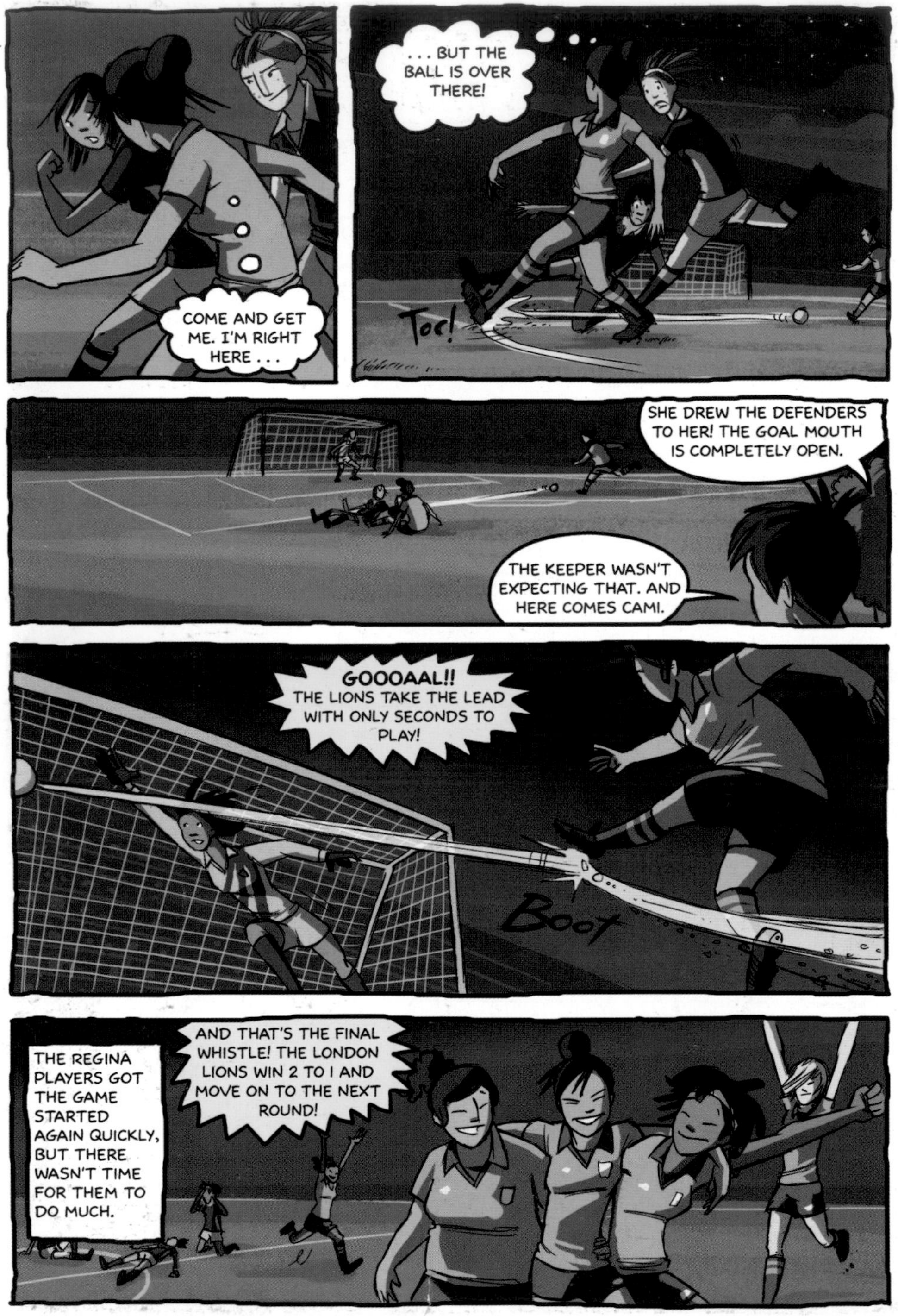
COME AND GET ME. I'M RIGHT HERE . . .
. . . BUT THE BALL IS OVER THERE!
TOC!
SHE DREW THE DEFENDERS TO HER! THE GOAL MOUTH IS COMPLETELY OPEN.
THE KEEPER WASN'T EXPECTING THAT. AND HERE COMES CAMI.
GOOOAAL!! THE LIONS TAKE THE LEAD WITH ONLY SECONDS TO PLAY!
BOOT
THE REGINA PLAYERS GOT THE GAME STARTED AGAIN QUICKLY, BUT THERE WASN'T TIME FOR THEM TO DO MUCH.
AND THAT'S THE FINAL WHISTLE! THE LONDON LIONS WIN 2 TO 1 AND MOVE ON TO THE NEXT ROUND!

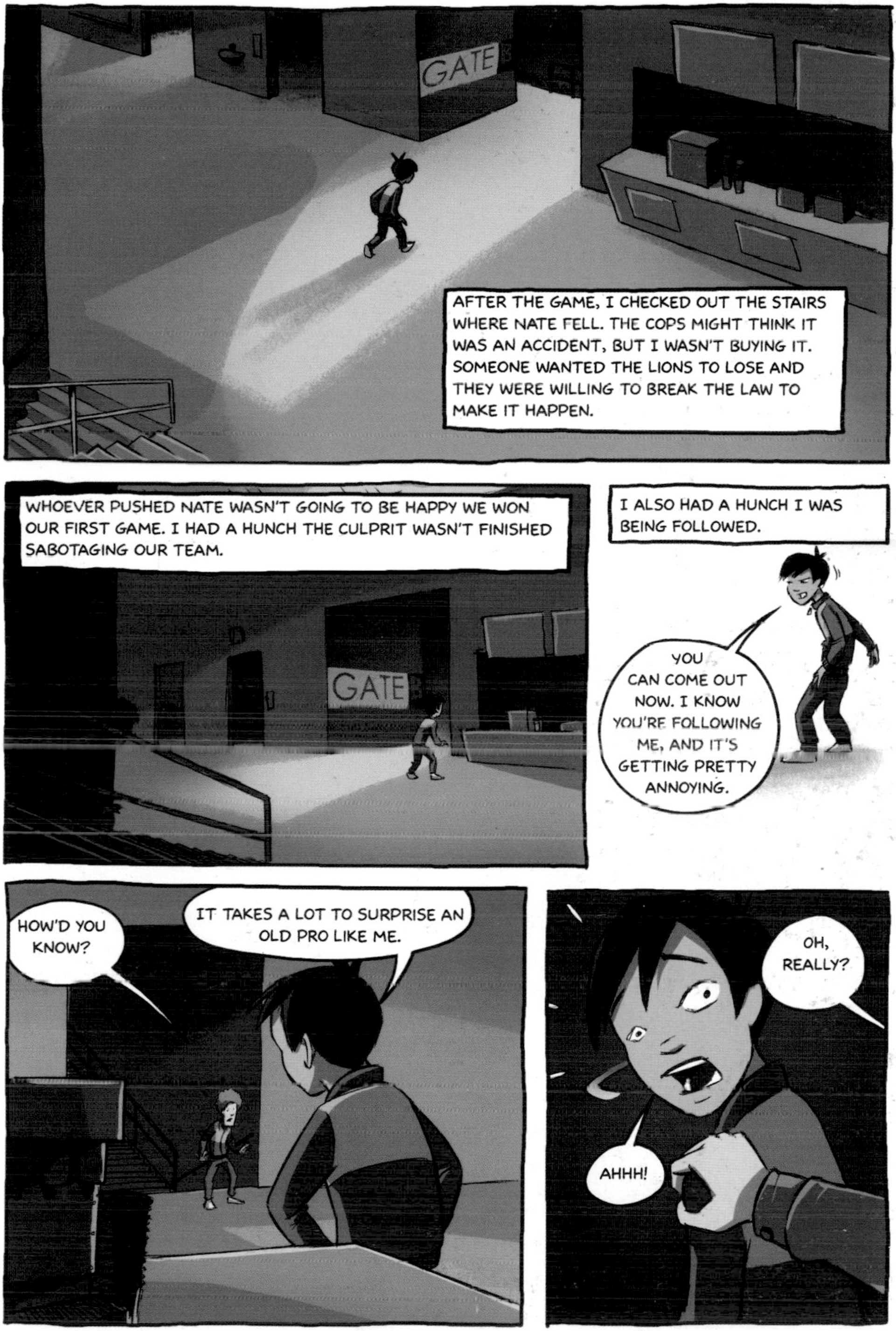
AFTER THE GAME, I CHECKED OUT THE STAIRS WHERE NATE FELL. THE COPS MIGHT THINK IT WAS AN ACCIDENT, BUT I WASN'T BUYING IT. SOMEONE WANTED THE LIONS TO LOSE AND THEY WERE WILLING TO BREAK THE LAW TO MAKE IT HAPPEN.
GATE
WHOEVER PUSHED NATE WASN'T GOING TO BE HAPPY WE WON OUR FIRST GAME. I HAD A HUNCH THE CULPRIT WASN'T FINISHED SABOTAGING OUR TEAM.
GATE
I ALSO HAD A HUNCH I WAS BEING FOLLOWED.
YOU CAN COME OUT NOW. I KNOW YOU'RE FOLLOWING ME, AND IT'S GETTING PRETTY ANNOYING.
HOW'D YOU KNOW?
IT TAKES A LOT TO SURPRISE AN OLD PRO LIKE ME.
OH, REALLY?
AHHH!

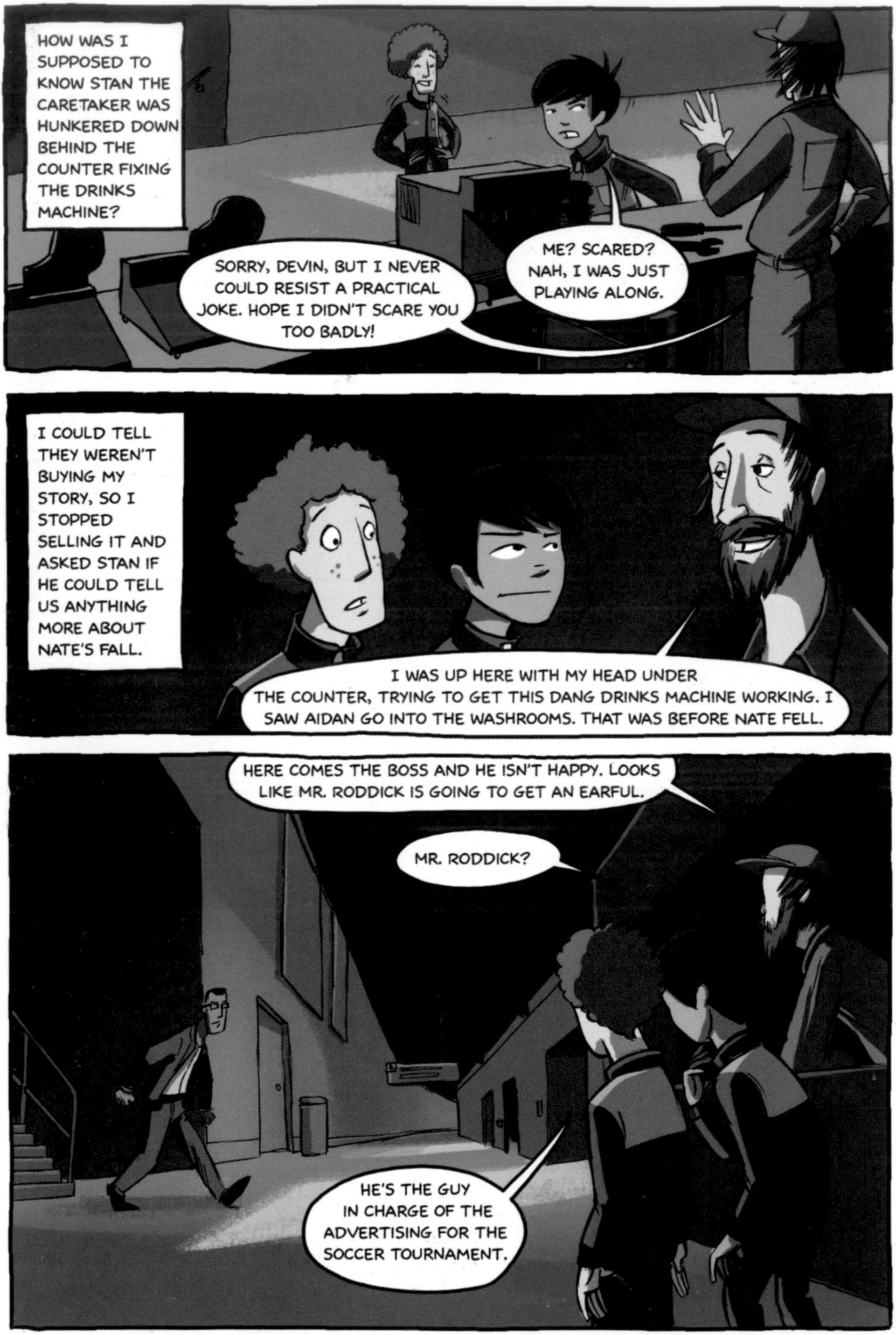
HOW WAS I SUPPOSED TO KNOW STAN THE CARETAKER WAS HUNKERED DOWN BEHIND THE COUNTER FIXING THE DRINKS MACHINE?
SORRY, DEVIN, BUT I NEVER COULD RESIST A PRACTICAL JOKE. HOPE I DIDN'T SCARE YOU TOO BADLY!
ME? SCARED? NAH, I WAS JUST PLAYING ALONG.
I COULD TELL THEY WEREN'T BUYING MY STORY, SO I STOPPED SELLING IT AND ASKED STAN IF HE COULD TELL US ANYTHING MORE ABOUT NATE'S FALL.
I WAS UP HERE WITH MY HEAD UNDER THE COUNTER, TRYING TO GET THIS DANG DRINKS MACHINE WORKING. I SAW AIDAN GO INTO THE WASHROOMS. THAT WAS BEFORE NATE FELL.
HERE COMES THE BOSS AND HE ISN'T HAPPY. LOOKS LIKE MR. RODDICK IS GOING TO GET AN EARFUL.
MR. RODDICK?
HE'S THE GUY IN CHARGE OF THE ADVERTISING FOR THE SOCCER TOURNAMENT.

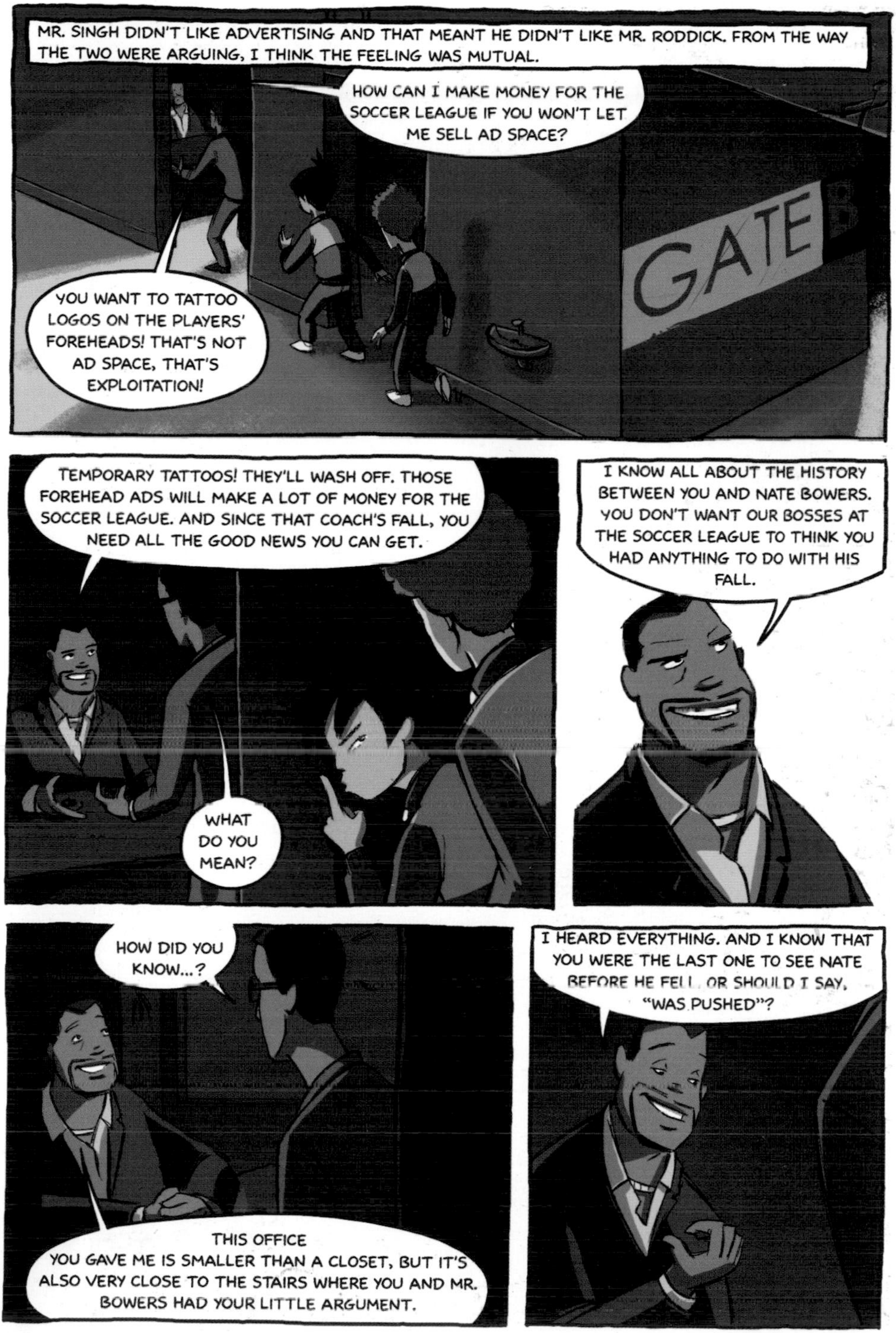
MR. SINGH DIDN'T LIKE ADVERTISING AND THAT MEANT HE DIDN'T LIKE MR. RODDICK. FROM THE WAY THE TWO WERE ARGUING, I THINK THE FEELING WAS MUTUAL.
HOW CAN I MAKE MONEY FOR THE SOCCER LEAGUE IF YOU WON'T LET ME SELL AD SPACE?
YOU WANT TO TATTOO LOGOS ON THE PLAYERS' FOREHEADS! THAT'S NOT AD SPACE, THAT'S EXPLOITATION!
GATE
TEMPORARY TATTOOS! THEY'LL WASH OFF. THOSE FOREHEAD ADS WILL MAKE A LOT OF MONEY FOR THE SOCCER LEAGUE. AND SINCE THAT COACH'S FALL, YOU NEED ALL THE GOOD NEWS YOU CAN GET.
WHAT DO YOU MEAN?
I KNOW ALL ABOUT THE HISTORY BETWEEN YOU AND NATE BOWERS. YOU DON'T WANT OUR BOSSES AT THE SOCCER LEAGUE TO THINK YOU HAD ANYTHING TO DO WITH HIS FALL.
HOW DID YOU KNOW...?
THIS OFFICE YOU GAVE ME IS SMALLER THAN A CLOSET, BUT IT'S ALSO VERY CLOSE TO THE STAIRS WHERE YOU AND MR. BOWERS HAD YOUR LITTLE ARGUMENT.
I HEARD EVERYTHING. AND I KNOW THAT YOU WERE THE LAST ONE TO SEE NATE BEFORE HE FELL, OR SHOULD I SAY, "WAS PUSHED"?

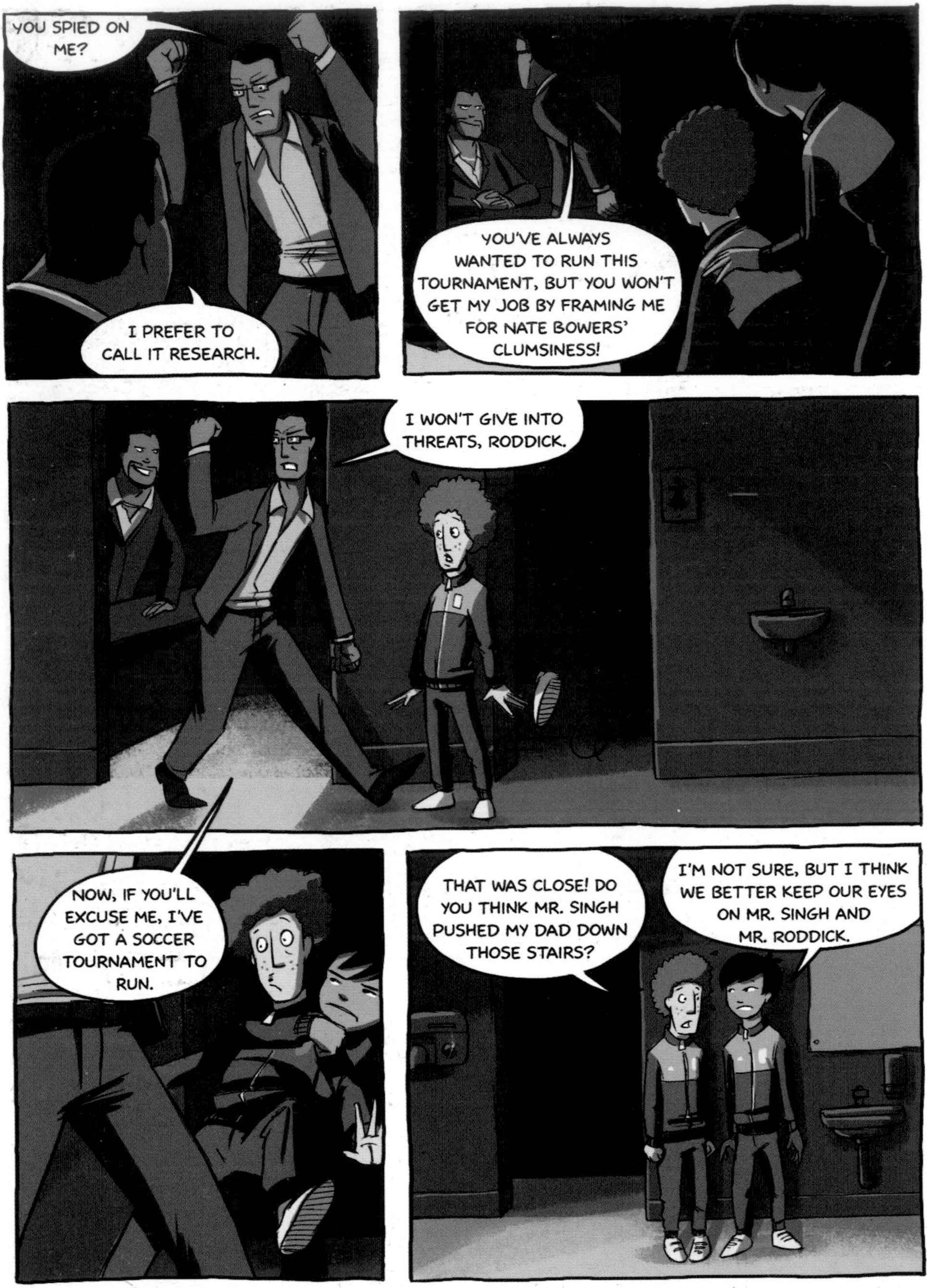
YOU SPIED ON ME?
I PREFER TO CALL IT RESEARCH.
YOU'VE ALWAYS WANTED TO RUN THIS TOURNAMENT, BUT YOU WON'T GET MY JOB BY FRAMING ME FOR NATE BOWERS' CLUMSINESS!
I WON'T GIVE INTO THREATS, RODDICK.
NOW, IF YOU'LL EXCUSE ME, I'VE GOT A SOCCER TOURNAMENT TO RUN.
THAT WAS CLOSE! DO YOU THINK MR. SINGH PUSHED MY DAD DOWN THOSE STAIRS?
I'M NOT SURE, BUT I THINK WE BETTER KEEP OUR EYES ON MR. SINGH AND MR. RODDICK.

CHAPTER 3

CLUES FROM THE PAST

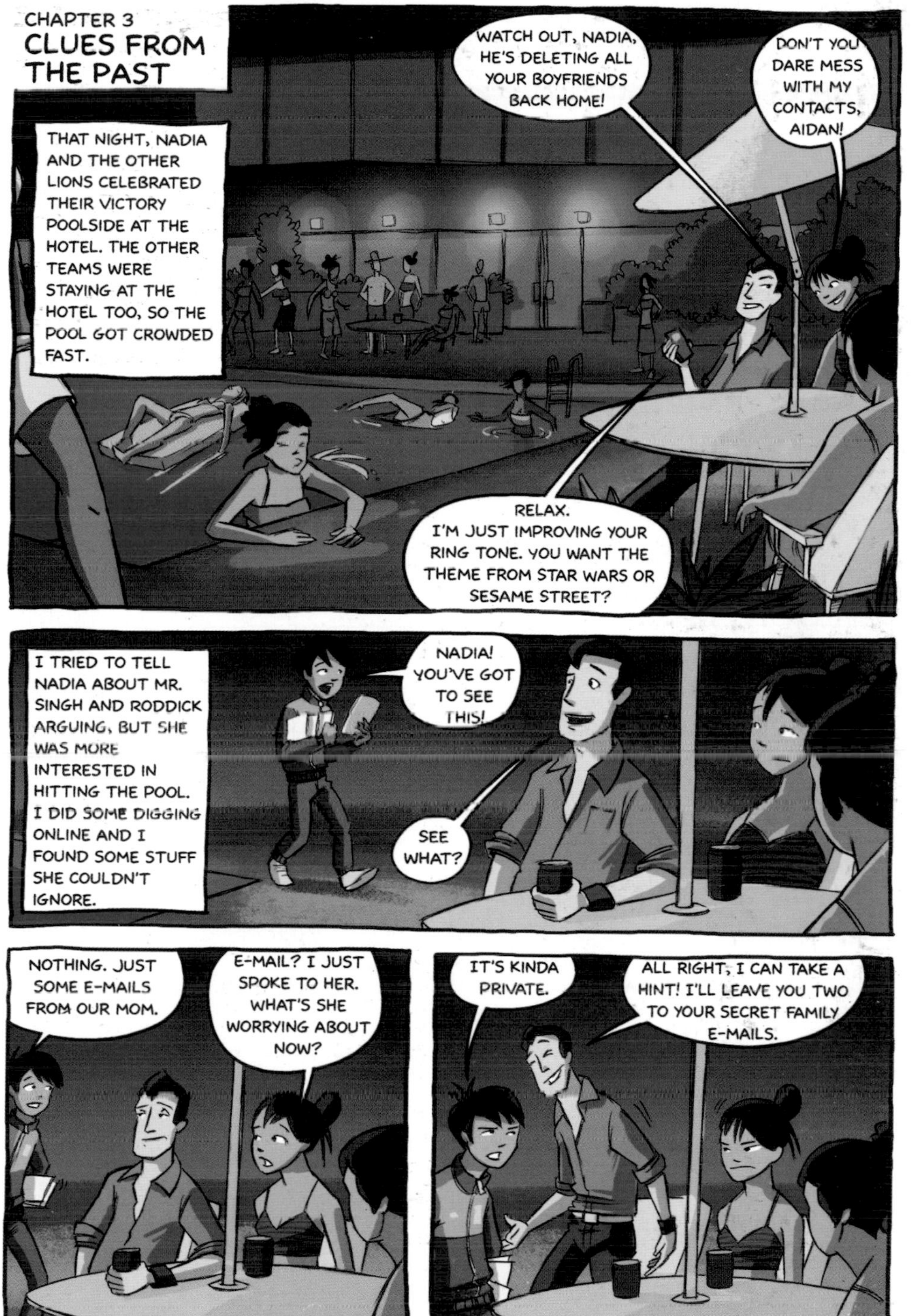

THAT NIGHT, NADIA AND THE OTHER LIONS CELEBRATED THEIR VICTORY POOLSIDE AT THE HOTEL. THE OTHER TEAMS WERE STAYING AT THE HOTEL TOO, SO THE POOL GOT CROWDED FAST.
WATCH OUT, NADIA, HE'S DELETING ALL YOUR BOYFRIENDS BACK HOME!
DON'T YOU DARE MESS WITH MY CONTACTS, AIDAN!
RELAX. I'M JUST IMPROVING YOUR RING TONE. YOU WANT THE THEME FROM STAR WARS OR SESAME STREET?
I TRIED TO TELL NADIA ABOUT MR. SINGH AND RODDICK ARGUING, BUT SHE WAS MORE INTERESTED IN HITTING THE POOL. I DID SOME DIGGING ONLINE AND I FOUND SOME STUFF SHE COULDN'T IGNORE.
NADIA! YOU'VE GOT TO SEE THIS!
SEE WHAT?
NOTHING. JUST SOME E-MAILS FROM OUR MOM.
E-MAIL? I JUST SPOKE TO HER. WHAT'S SHE WORRYING ABOUT NOW?
IT'S KINDA PRIVATE.
ALL RIGHT, I CAN TAKE A HINT! I'LL LEAVE YOU TWO TO YOUR SECRET FAMILY E-MAILS.

OKAY, DEVIN, WHAT'S REALLY UP? I JUST CHECKED MY E-MAIL. MOM HASN'T SENT ANYTHING. WHATEVER YOU'VE GOT, IT ISN'T FROM HER.

YOU'RE RIGHT, BUT I HAD TO GET RID OF YOUR BOYFRIEND SOMEHOW.

OUCH! SCORE ONE FOR LITTLE D-MAN!

NADIA STILL THOUGHT NATE'S FALL WAS AN ACCIDENT. EVEN AFTER I TOLD HER ABOUT MR. RODDICK THREATENING MR. SINGH. I HOPED THE OLD ARTICLES I FOUND WOULD CHANGE HER MIND.

MR. SINGH AND NATE HAVE KNOWN EACH OTHER FOR YEARS. AND THEY WEREN'T THE BEST OF FRIENDS.

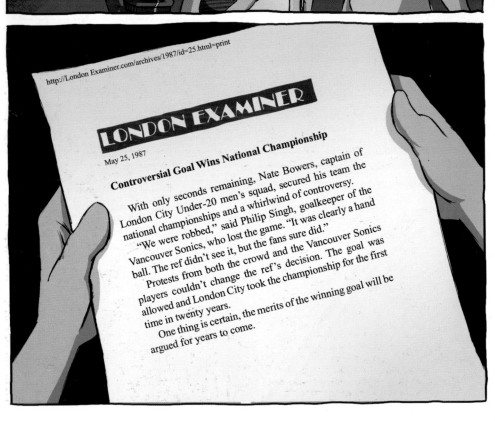

http://London Examiner.com/archives/1987/id=25.html=print

LONDON EXAMINER

May 25, 1987

Controversial Goal Wins National Championship

With only seconds remaining, Nate Bowers, captain of London City Under-20 men's squad, secured his team the national championships and a whirlwind of controversy.

"We were robbed," said Philip Singh, goalkeeper of the Vancouver Sonics, who lost the game. "It was clearly a hand ball. The ref didn't see it, but the fans sure did."

Protests from both the crowd and the Vancouver Sonics players couldn't change the ref's decision. The goal was allowed and London City took the championship for the first time in twenty years.

One thing is certain, the merits of the winning goal will be argued for years to come.

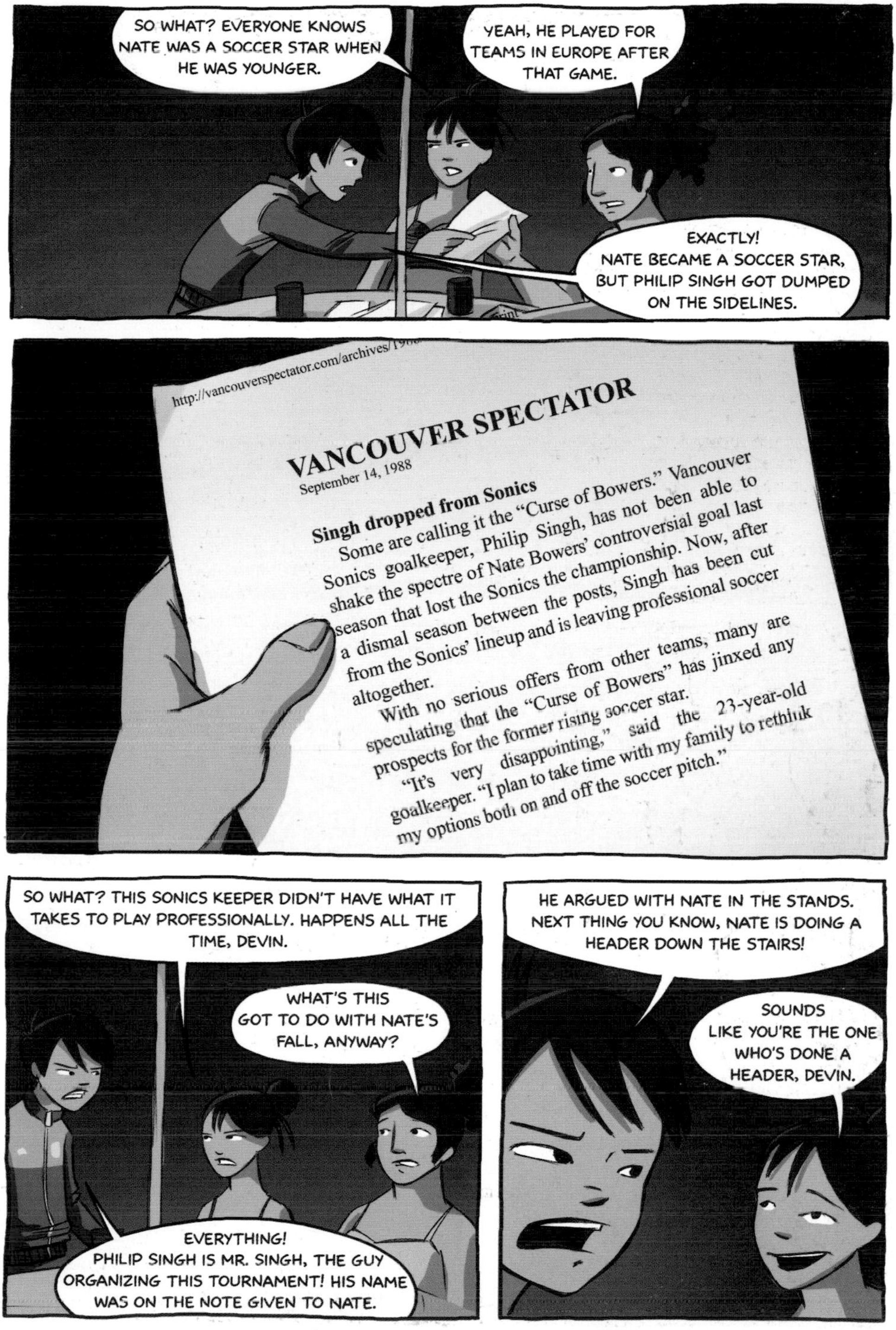
SO WHAT? EVERYONE KNOWS NATE WAS A SOCCER STAR WHEN HE WAS YOUNGER.
YEAH, HE PLAYED FOR TEAMS IN EUROPE AFTER THAT GAME.
EXACTLY! NATE BECAME A SOCCER STAR, BUT PHILIP SINGH GOT DUMPED ON THE SIDELINES.
http://vancouverspectator.com/archives/19
VANCOUVER SPECTATOR
September 14, 1988
Singh dropped from Sonics
Some are calling it the "Curse of Bowers." Vancouver Sonics goalkeeper, Philip Singh, has not been able to shake the spectre of Nate Bowers' controversial goal last season that lost the Sonics the championship. Now, after a dismal season between the posts, Singh has been cut from the Sonics' lineup and is leaving professional soccer altogether.
With no serious offers from other teams, many are speculating that the "Curse of Bowers" has jinxed any prospects for the former rising soccer star.
"It's very disappointing," said the 23-year-old goalkeeper. "I plan to take time with my family to rethink my options both on and off the soccer pitch."
SO WHAT? THIS SONICS KEEPER DIDN'T HAVE WHAT IT TAKES TO PLAY PROFESSIONALLY. HAPPENS ALL THE TIME, DEVIN.
WHAT'S THIS GOT TO DO WITH NATE'S FALL, ANYWAY?
EVERYTHING! PHILIP SINGH IS MR. SINGH, THE GUY ORGANIZING THIS TOURNAMENT! HIS NAME WAS ON THE NOTE GIVEN TO NATE.
HE ARGUED WITH NATE IN THE STANDS. NEXT THING YOU KNOW, NATE IS DOING A HEADER DOWN THE STAIRS!
SOUNDS LIKE YOU'RE THE ONE WHO'S DONE A HEADER, DEVIN.

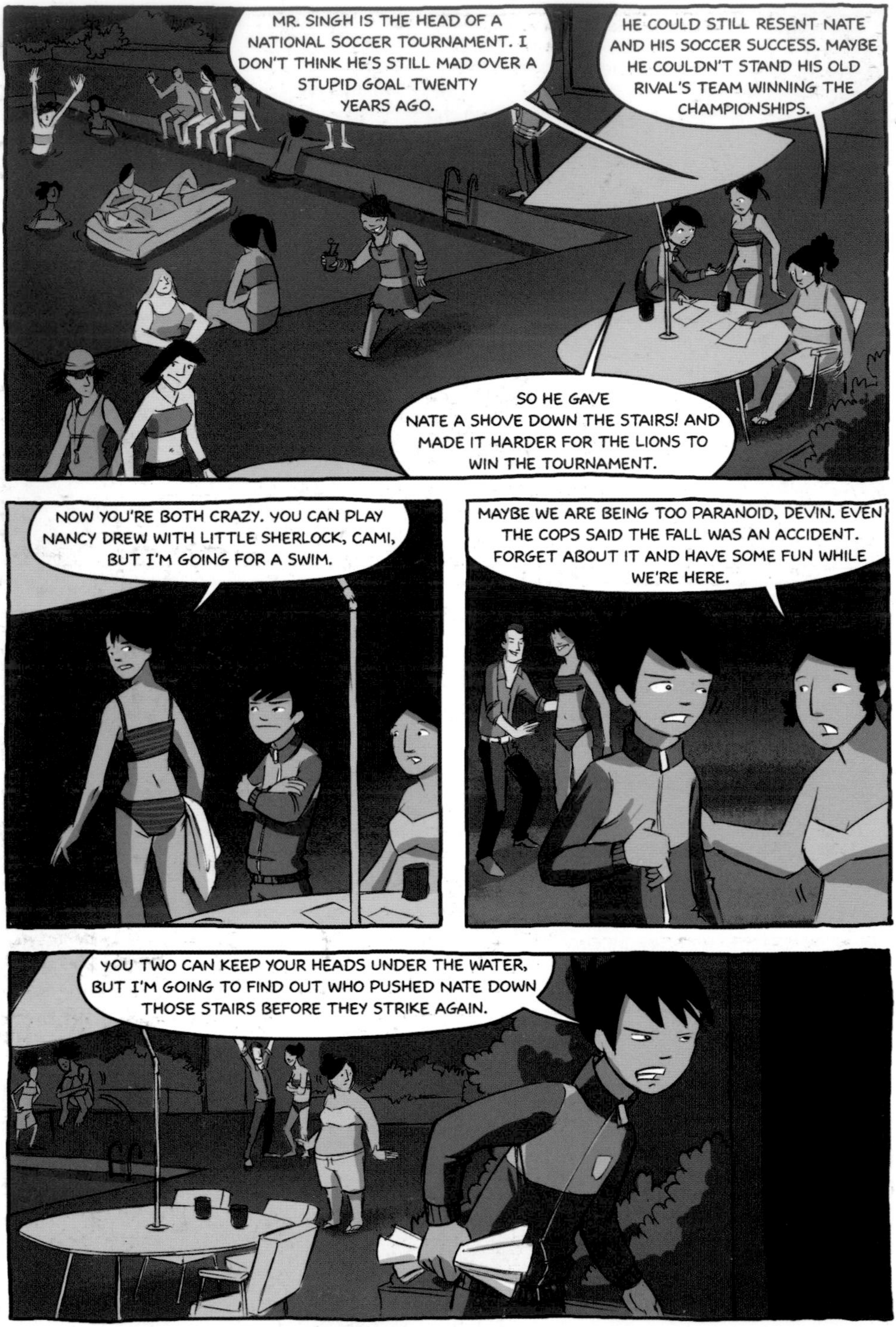
MR. SINGH IS THE HEAD OF A NATIONAL SOCCER TOURNAMENT. I DON'T THINK HE'S STILL MAD OVER A STUPID GOAL TWENTY YEARS AGO.
HE COULD STILL RESENT NATE AND HIS SOCCER SUCCESS. MAYBE HE COULDN'T STAND HIS OLD RIVAL'S TEAM WINNING THE CHAMPIONSHIPS.
SO HE GAVE NATE A SHOVE DOWN THE STAIRS! AND MADE IT HARDER FOR THE LIONS TO WIN THE TOURNAMENT.
NOW YOU'RE BOTH CRAZY. YOU CAN PLAY NANCY DREW WITH LITTLE SHERLOCK, CAMI, BUT I'M GOING FOR A SWIM.
MAYBE WE ARE BEING TOO PARANOID, DEVIN. EVEN THE COPS SAID THE FALL WAS AN ACCIDENT. FORGET ABOUT IT AND HAVE SOME FUN WHILE WE'RE HERE.
YOU TWO CAN KEEP YOUR HEADS UNDER THE WATER, BUT I'M GOING TO FIND OUT WHO PUSHED NATE DOWN THOSE STAIRS BEFORE THEY STRIKE AGAIN.

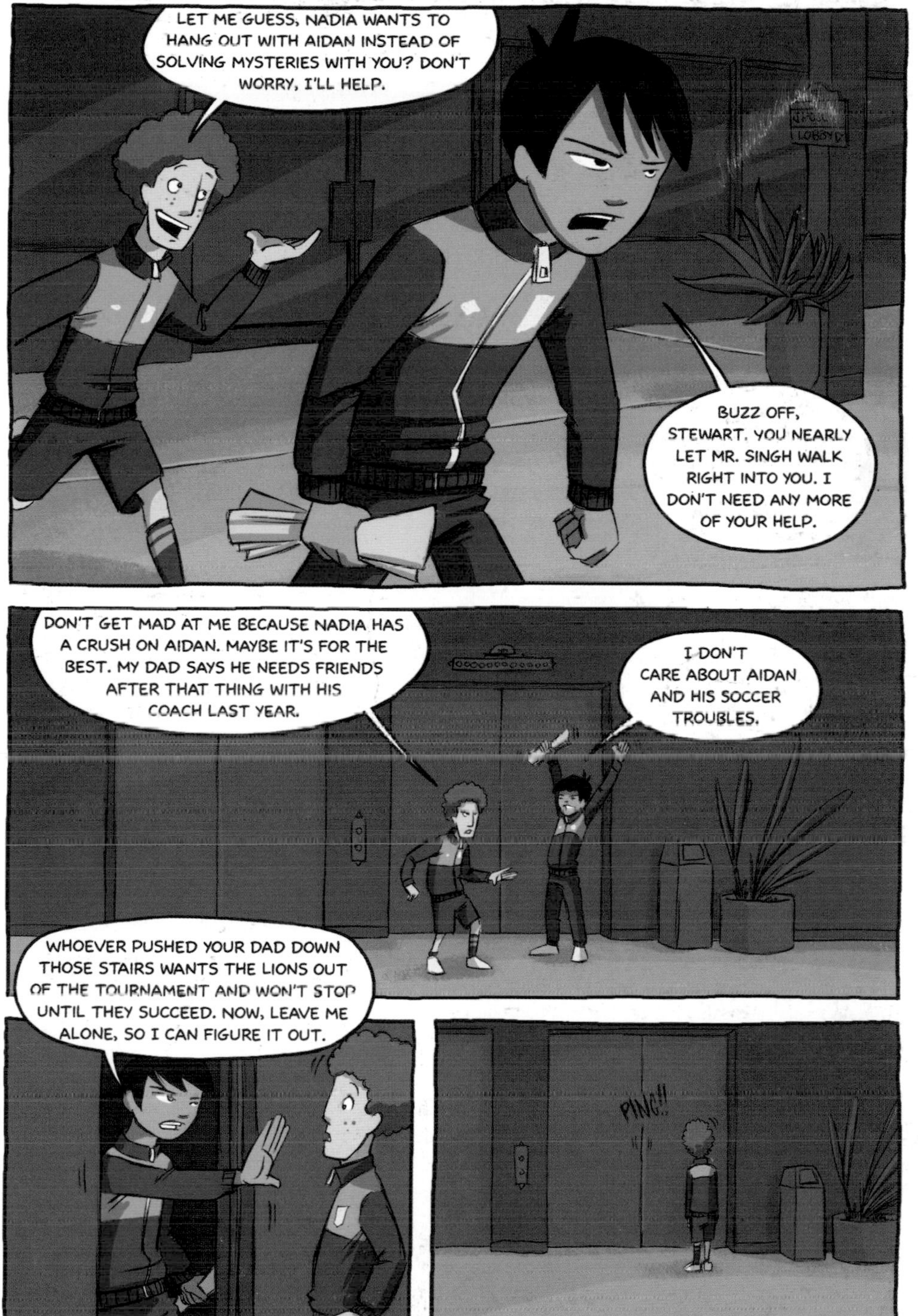
LET ME GUESS, NADIA WANTS TO HANG OUT WITH AIDAN INSTEAD OF SOLVING MYSTERIES WITH YOU? DON'T WORRY, I'LL HELP.
BUZZ OFF, STEWART. YOU NEARLY LET MR. SINGH WALK RIGHT INTO YOU. I DON'T NEED ANY MORE OF YOUR HELP.
DON'T GET MAD AT ME BECAUSE NADIA HAS A CRUSH ON AIDAN. MAYBE IT'S FOR THE BEST. MY DAD SAYS HE NEEDS FRIENDS AFTER THAT THING WITH HIS COACH LAST YEAR.
I DON'T CARE ABOUT AIDAN AND HIS SOCCER TROUBLES.
WHOEVER PUSHED YOUR DAD DOWN THOSE STAIRS WANTS THE LIONS OUT OF THE TOURNAMENT AND WON'T STOP UNTIL THEY SUCCEED. NOW, LEAVE ME ALONE, SO I CAN FIGURE IT OUT.
PING!!

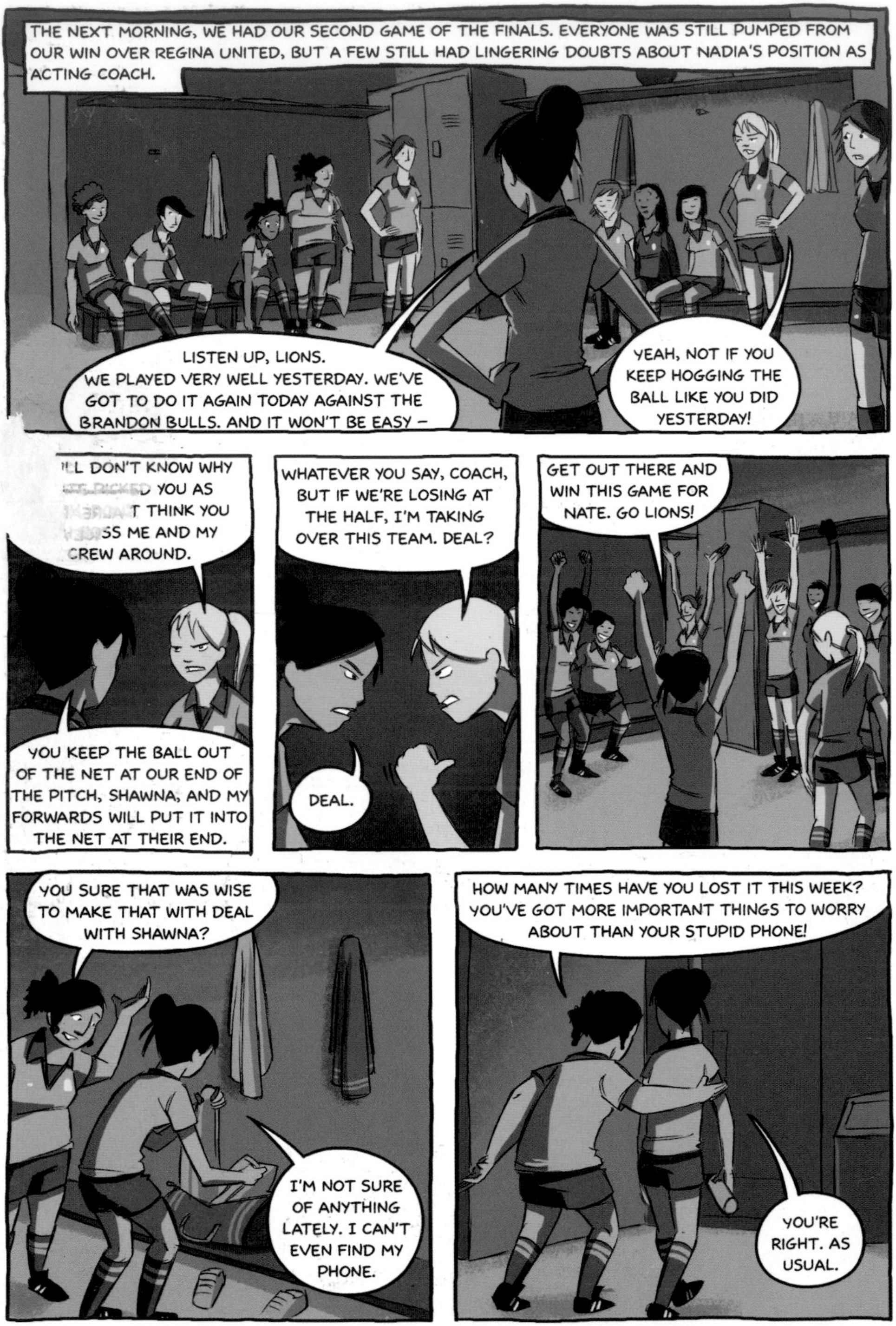
THE NEXT MORNING, WE HAD OUR SECOND GAME OF THE FINALS. EVERYONE WAS STILL PUMPED FROM OUR WIN OVER REGINA UNITED, BUT A FEW STILL HAD LINGERING DOUBTS ABOUT NADIA'S POSITION AS ACTING COACH.
LISTEN UP, LIONS. WE PLAYED VERY WELL YESTERDAY. WE'VE GOT TO DO IT AGAIN TODAY AGAINST THE BRANDON BULLS. AND IT WON'T BE EASY –
YEAH, NOT IF YOU KEEP HOGGING THE BALL LIKE YOU DID YESTERDAY!
LL DON'T KNOW WHY D YOU AS T THINK YOU SS ME AND MY CREW AROUND.
YOU KEEP THE BALL OUT OF THE NET AT OUR END OF THE PITCH, SHAWNA, AND MY FORWARDS WILL PUT IT INTO THE NET AT THEIR END.
WHATEVER YOU SAY, COACH, BUT IF WE'RE LOSING AT THE HALF, I'M TAKING OVER THIS TEAM. DEAL?
DEAL.
GET OUT THERE AND WIN THIS GAME FOR NATE. GO LIONS!
YOU SURE THAT WAS WISE TO MAKE THAT WITH DEAL WITH SHAWNA?
I'M NOT SURE OF ANYTHING LATELY. I CAN'T EVEN FIND MY PHONE.
HOW MANY TIMES HAVE YOU LOST IT THIS WEEK? YOU'VE GOT MORE IMPORTANT THINGS TO WORRY ABOUT THAN YOUR STUPID PHONE!
YOU'RE RIGHT. AS USUAL.

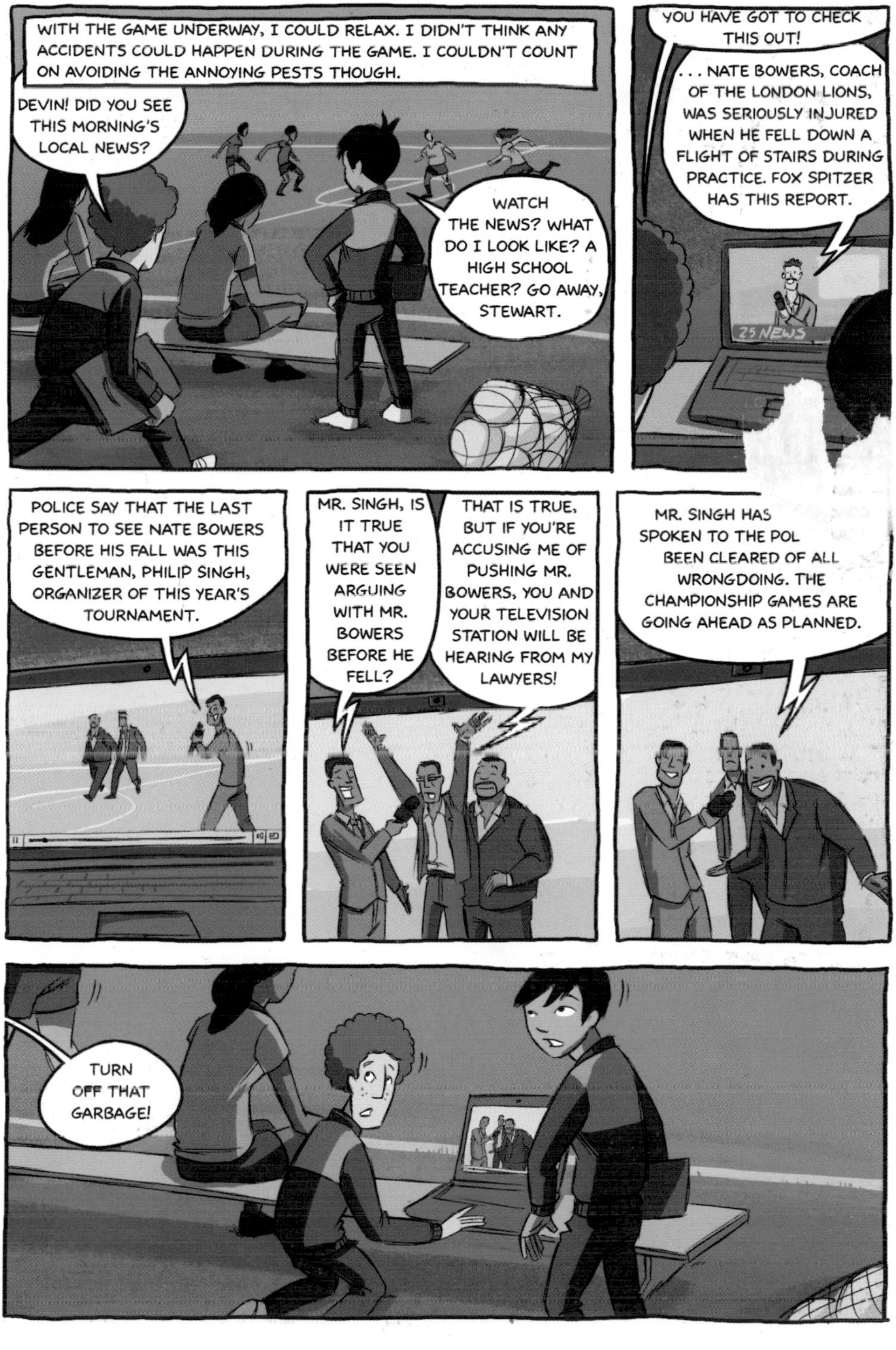

WITH THE GAME UNDERWAY, I COULD RELAX. I DIDN'T THINK ANY ACCIDENTS COULD HAPPEN DURING THE GAME. I COULDN'T COUNT ON AVOIDING THE ANNOYING PESTS THOUGH.
DEVIN! DID YOU SEE THIS MORNING'S LOCAL NEWS?
WATCH THE NEWS? WHAT DO I LOOK LIKE? A HIGH SCHOOL TEACHER? GO AWAY, STEWART.
YOU HAVE GOT TO CHECK THIS OUT!
. . . NATE BOWERS, COACH OF THE LONDON LIONS, WAS SERIOUSLY INJURED WHEN HE FELL DOWN A FLIGHT OF STAIRS DURING PRACTICE. FOX SPITZER HAS THIS REPORT.
25 NEWS
POLICE SAY THAT THE LAST PERSON TO SEE NATE BOWERS BEFORE HIS FALL WAS THIS GENTLEMAN, PHILIP SINGH, ORGANIZER OF THIS YEAR'S TOURNAMENT.
MR. SINGH, IS IT TRUE THAT YOU WERE SEEN ARGUING WITH MR. BOWERS BEFORE HE FELL?
THAT IS TRUE, BUT IF YOU'RE ACCUSING ME OF PUSHING MR. BOWERS, YOU AND YOUR TELEVISION STATION WILL BE HEARING FROM MY LAWYERS!
MR. SINGH HAS SPOKEN TO THE POL BEEN CLEARED OF ALL WRONGDOING. THE CHAMPIONSHIP GAMES ARE GOING AHEAD AS PLANNED.
TURN OFF THAT GARBAGE!

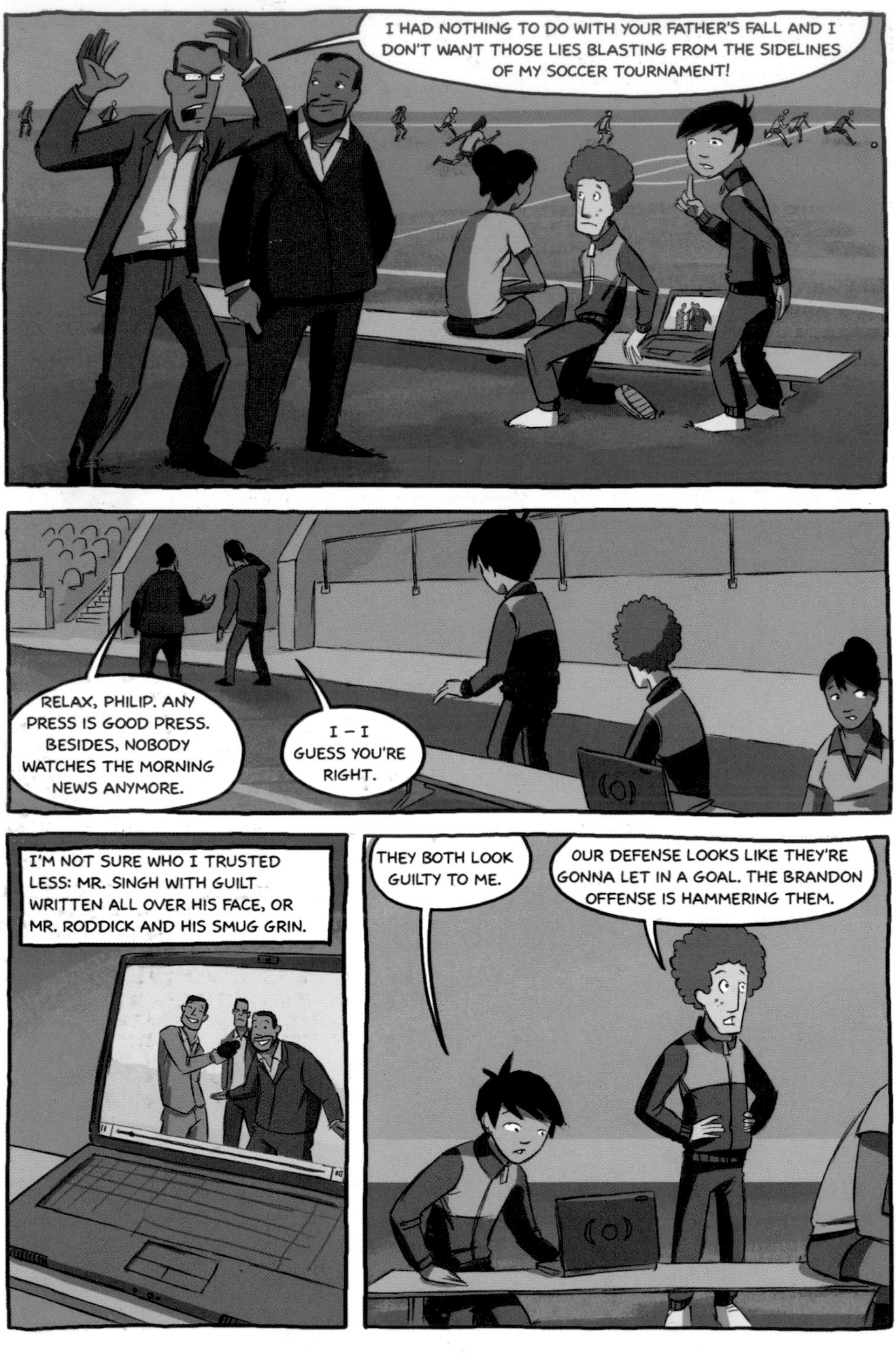
I HAD NOTHING TO DO WITH YOUR FATHER'S FALL AND I DON'T WANT THOSE LIES BLASTING FROM THE SIDELINES OF MY SOCCER TOURNAMENT!
RELAX, PHILIP. ANY PRESS IS GOOD PRESS. BESIDES, NOBODY WATCHES THE MORNING NEWS ANYMORE.
I – I GUESS YOU'RE RIGHT.
I'M NOT SURE WHO I TRUSTED LESS: MR. SINGH WITH GUILT WRITTEN ALL OVER HIS FACE, OR MR. RODDICK AND HIS SMUG GRIN.
THEY BOTH LOOK GUILTY TO ME.
OUR DEFENSE LOOKS LIKE THEY'RE GONNA LET IN A GOAL. THE BRANDON OFFENSE IS HAMMERING THEM.

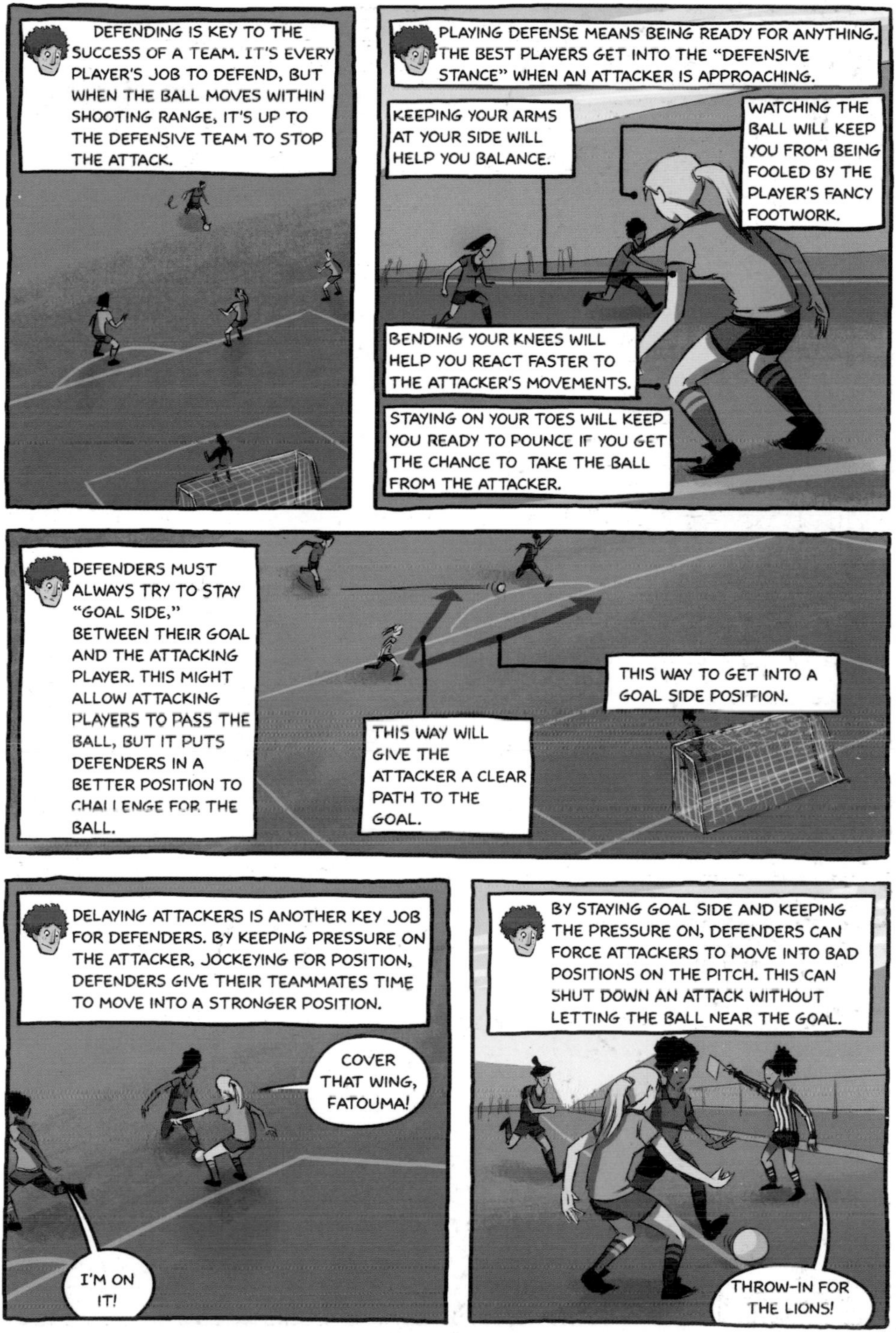
DEFENDING IS KEY TO THE SUCCESS OF A TEAM. IT'S EVERY PLAYER'S JOB TO DEFEND, BUT WHEN THE BALL MOVES WITHIN SHOOTING RANGE, IT'S UP TO THE DEFENSIVE TEAM TO STOP THE ATTACK.
PLAYING DEFENSE MEANS BEING READY FOR ANYTHING. THE BEST PLAYERS GET INTO THE "DEFENSIVE STANCE" WHEN AN ATTACKER IS APPROACHING.
KEEPING YOUR ARMS AT YOUR SIDE WILL HELP YOU BALANCE.
WATCHING THE BALL WILL KEEP YOU FROM BEING FOOLED BY THE PLAYER'S FANCY FOOTWORK.
BENDING YOUR KNEES WILL HELP YOU REACT FASTER TO THE ATTACKER'S MOVEMENTS.
STAYING ON YOUR TOES WILL KEEP YOU READY TO POUNCE IF YOU GET THE CHANCE TO TAKE THE BALL FROM THE ATTACKER.
DEFENDERS MUST ALWAYS TRY TO STAY "GOAL SIDE," BETWEEN THEIR GOAL AND THE ATTACKING PLAYER. THIS MIGHT ALLOW ATTACKING PLAYERS TO PASS THE BALL, BUT IT PUTS DEFENDERS IN A BETTER POSITION TO CHALLENGE FOR THE BALL.
THIS WAY TO GET INTO A GOAL SIDE POSITION.
THIS WAY WILL GIVE THE ATTACKER A CLEAR PATH TO THE GOAL.
DELAYING ATTACKERS IS ANOTHER KEY JOB FOR DEFENDERS. BY KEEPING PRESSURE ON THE ATTACKER, JOCKEYING FOR POSITION, DEFENDERS GIVE THEIR TEAMMATES TIME TO MOVE INTO A STRONGER POSITION.
COVER THAT WING, FATOUMA!
I'M ON IT!
BY STAYING GOAL SIDE AND KEEPING THE PRESSURE ON, DEFENDERS CAN FORCE ATTACKERS TO MOVE INTO BAD POSITIONS ON THE PITCH. THIS CAN SHUT DOWN AN ATTACK WITHOUT LETTING THE BALL NEAR THE GOAL.
THROW-IN FOR THE LIONS!

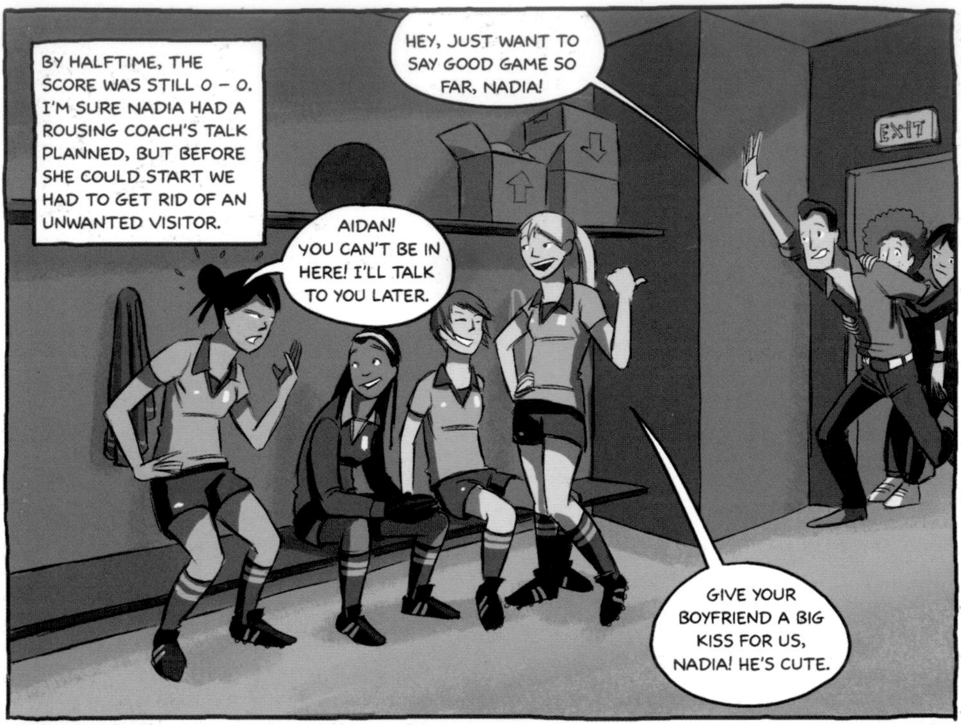
BY HALFTIME, THE SCORE WAS STILL 0 – 0. I'M SURE NADIA HAD A ROUSING COACH'S TALK PLANNED, BUT BEFORE SHE COULD START WE HAD TO GET RID OF AN UNWANTED VISITOR.
HEY, JUST WANT TO SAY GOOD GAME SO FAR, NADIA!
EXIT
AIDAN! YOU CAN'T BE IN HERE! I'LL TALK TO YOU LATER.
GIVE YOUR BOYFRIEND A BIG KISS FOR US, NADIA! HE'S CUTE.

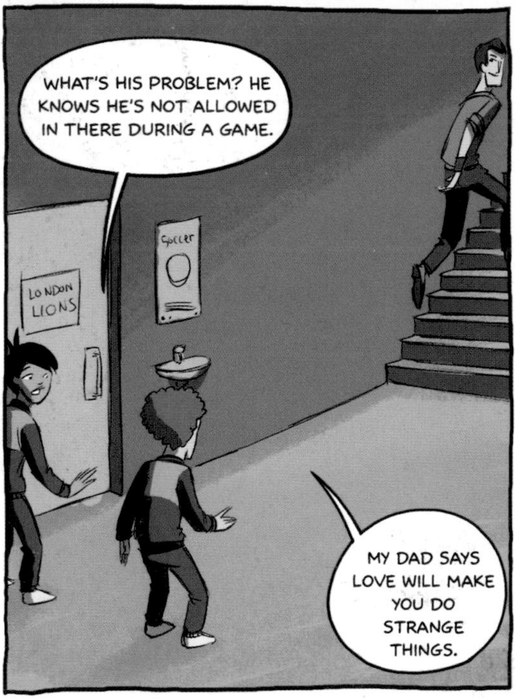
WHAT'S HIS PROBLEM? HE KNOWS HE'S NOT ALLOWED IN THERE DURING A GAME.
Soccer
LONDON LIONS
MY DAD SAYS LOVE WILL MAKE YOU DO STRANGE THINGS.

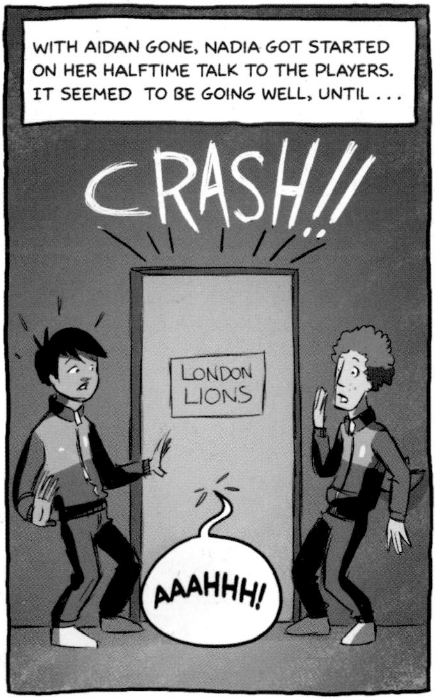
WITH AIDAN GONE, NADIA GOT STARTED ON HER HALFTIME TALK TO THE PLAYERS. IT SEEMED TO BE GOING WELL, UNTIL . . .
CRASH!!
LONDON LIONS
AAAHHH!

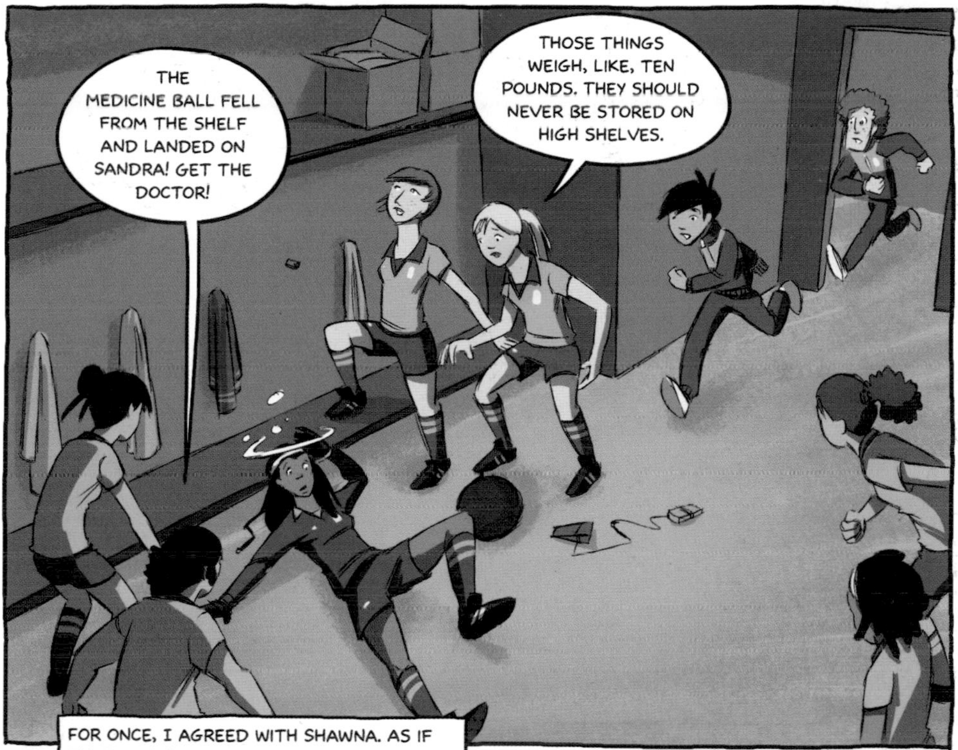
THE MEDICINE BALL FELL FROM THE SHELF AND LANDED ON SANDRA! GET THE DOCTOR!
THOSE THINGS WEIGH, LIKE, TEN POUNDS. THEY SHOULD NEVER BE STORED ON HIGH SHELVES.

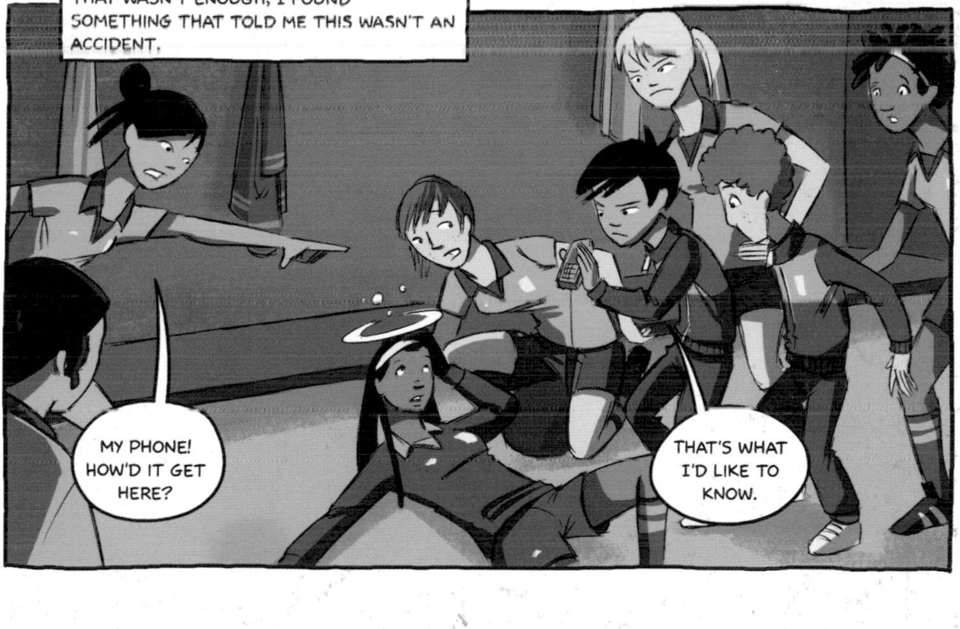
FOR ONCE, I AGREED WITH SHAWNA. AS IF THAT WASN'T ENOUGH, I FOUND SOMETHING THAT TOLD ME THIS WASN'T AN ACCIDENT.
MY PHONE! HOW'D IT GET HERE?
THAT'S WHAT I'D LIKE TO KNOW.

CHAPTER 4

TRACKING THE MYSTERY CALLER

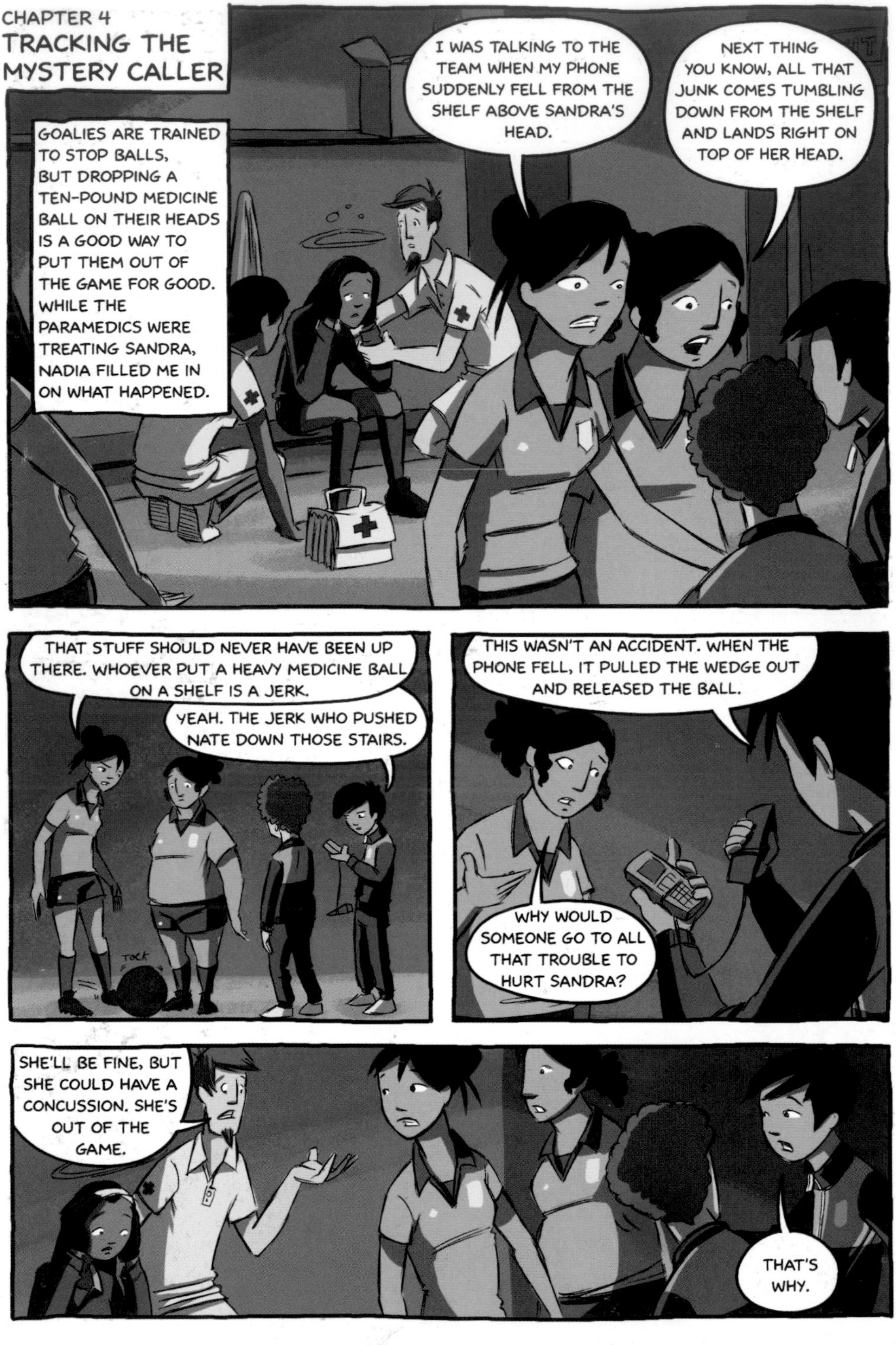
GOALIES ARE TRAINED TO STOP BALLS, BUT DROPPING A TEN-POUND MEDICINE BALL ON THEIR HEADS IS A GOOD WAY TO PUT THEM OUT OF THE GAME FOR GOOD. WHILE THE PARAMEDICS WERE TREATING SANDRA, NADIA FILLED ME IN ON WHAT HAPPENED.
I WAS TALKING TO THE TEAM WHEN MY PHONE SUDDENLY FELL FROM THE SHELF ABOVE SANDRA'S HEAD.
NEXT THING YOU KNOW, ALL THAT JUNK COMES TUMBLING DOWN FROM THE SHELF AND LANDS RIGHT ON TOP OF HER HEAD.
THAT STUFF SHOULD NEVER HAVE BEEN UP THERE. WHOEVER PUT A HEAVY MEDICINE BALL ON A SHELF IS A JERK.
YEAH. THE JERK WHO PUSHED NATE DOWN THOSE STAIRS.
TOCK
THIS WASN'T AN ACCIDENT. WHEN THE PHONE FELL, IT PULLED THE WEDGE OUT AND RELEASED THE BALL.
WHY WOULD SOMEONE GO TO ALL THAT TROUBLE TO HURT SANDRA?
SHE'LL BE FINE, BUT SHE COULD HAVE A CONCUSSION. SHE'S OUT OF THE GAME.
THAT'S WHY.

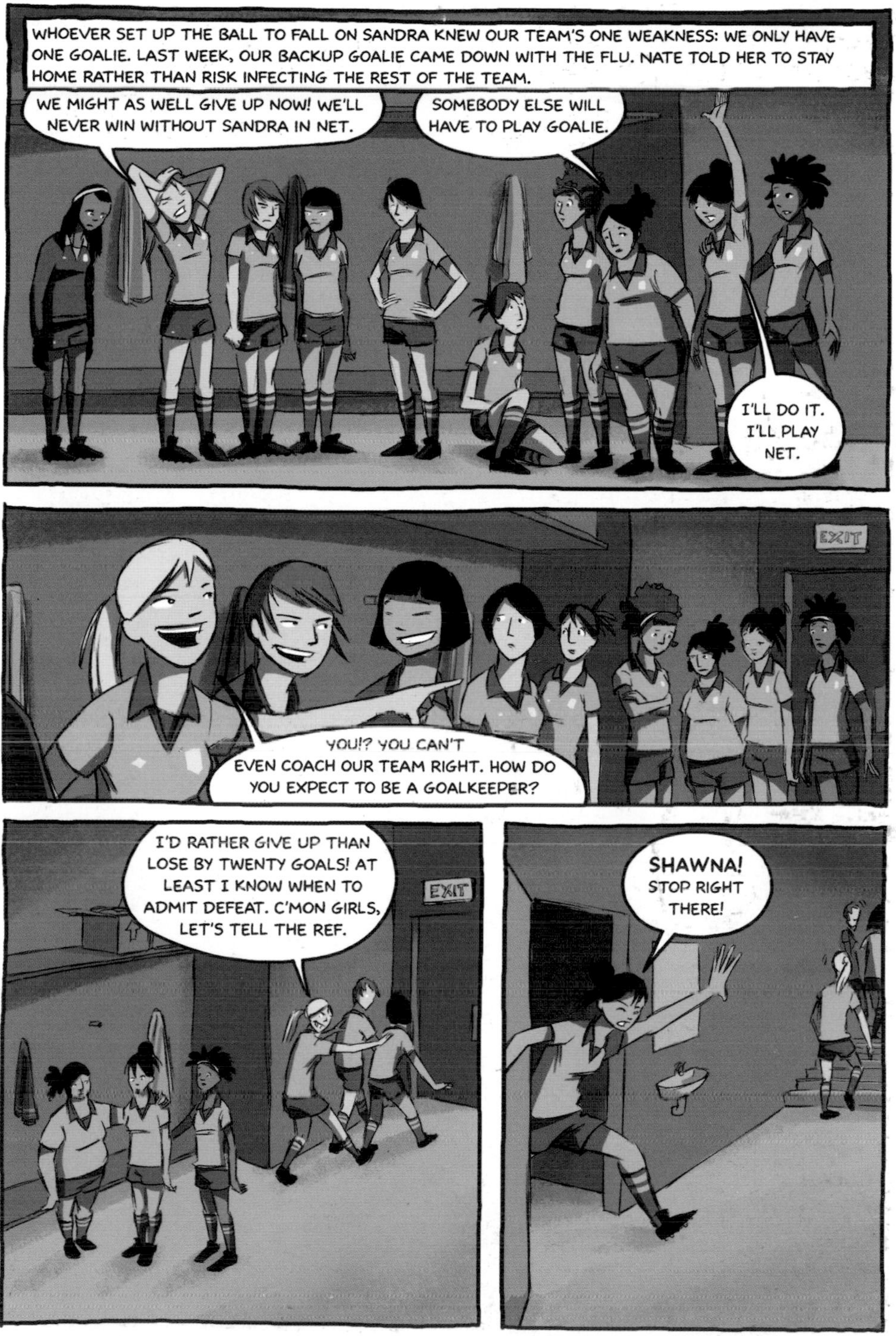
WHOEVER SET UP THE BALL TO FALL ON SANDRA KNEW OUR TEAM'S ONE WEAKNESS: WE ONLY HAVE ONE GOALIE. LAST WEEK, OUR BACKUP GOALIE CAME DOWN WITH THE FLU. NATE TOLD HER TO STAY HOME RATHER THAN RISK INFECTING THE REST OF THE TEAM.
WE MIGHT AS WELL GIVE UP NOW! WE'LL NEVER WIN WITHOUT SANDRA IN NET.
SOMEBODY ELSE WILL HAVE TO PLAY GOALIE.
I'LL DO IT. I'LL PLAY NET.
EXIT
YOU!? YOU CAN'T EVEN COACH OUR TEAM RIGHT. HOW DO YOU EXPECT TO BE A GOALKEEPER?
I'D RATHER GIVE UP THAN LOSE BY TWENTY GOALS! AT LEAST I KNOW WHEN TO ADMIT DEFEAT. C'MON GIRLS, LET'S TELL THE REF.
EXIT
SHAWNA! STOP RIGHT THERE!

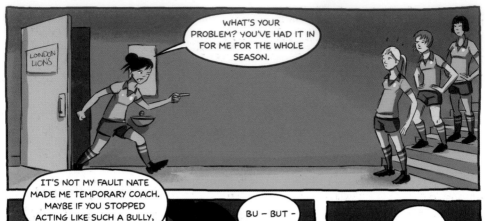

WHAT'S YOUR PROBLEM? YOU'VE HAD IT IN FOR ME FOR THE WHOLE SEASON.

IT'S NOT MY FAULT NATE MADE ME TEMPORARY COACH. MAYBE IF YOU STOPPED ACTING LIKE SUCH A BULLY, HE'D HAVE PICKED YOU.

BU – BUT –

I'M IN CHARGE, NOT YOU, SHAWNA. WE'RE A TEAM AND WE HAVE TO WORK TOGETHER. QUIT COMPLAINING AND HELP US WIN THIS GAME.

O – OKAY.

TRUCE?

TRUCE.

YAAAH!!

SO, YOU GOING TO SHOW ME HOW TO PLAY GOALKEEPER OR WHAT?

THE SECOND HALF IS ABOUT TO START, SO LET'S JUST GO OVER THE BASICS OF GOALKEEPING.

FAST FOOTWORK IS VITAL FOR A GOALKEEPER TO GET INTO POSITION TO STOP A SHOT. WHEN A PLAYER IS ABOUT TO TAKE A SHOT, THE KEEPER SHOULD BE READY.

EYES ON THE BALL AND NOT THE PLAYER.

HANDS UP AND READY TO CATCH THE BALL.

BODY SQUARE TO THE ATTACKING PLAYER, WITH THE KNEES AND HIPS FACING THE BALL.

KNEES BENT AND WEIGHT FORWARD, READY TO SPRING INTO ACTION.

CATCHING THE BALL IS THE BEST WAY FOR A GOALKEEPER TO STOP AN ATTACK. USE BOTH HANDS TO CATCH THE BALL. GET AS MUCH OF YOUR BODY BEHIND THE BALL.

Boot!

THAT'S IT! BRING THE BALL INTO YOUR CHEST TO CUSHION THE IMPACT AND CONTROL THE BALL.

A DIVING SAVE IS A GOALKEEPER'S LAST RESORT. KEEPERS SHOULD DIVE TO THE SIDE AND OUT FROM THE NET TOWARD THE BALL, TO GIVE THEMSELVES THE BEST ANGLE TO DEFLECT THE BALL.

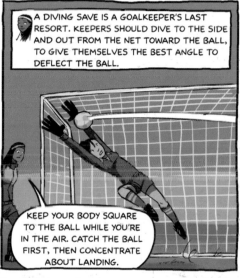

KEEP YOUR BODY SQUARE TO THE BALL WHILE YOU'RE IN THE AIR. CATCH THE BALL FIRST, THEN CONCENTRATE ABOUT LANDING.

RUNNING OUT TO MEET AN ATTACKING PLAYER NARROWS THE ANGLE THEY HAVE TO MAKE THE SHOT. STAY ON YOUR FEET FOR AS LONG AS YOU CAN.

ONLY DIVE WHEN THE SAVE MUST BE MADE. PLAYERS CAN EASILY DRIBBLE PAST A KEEPER WHO HAS FALLEN TO THE GROUND TOO EARLY.

SAFE AREA

THAT'S ABOUT ALL WE CAN SHOW YOU. THE REF'S ABOUT TO START THE GAME.

I HOPE I REMEMBER IT ALL.

YOU'LL BE FINE. WE'LL WORK TOGETHER TO WIN THIS GAME.

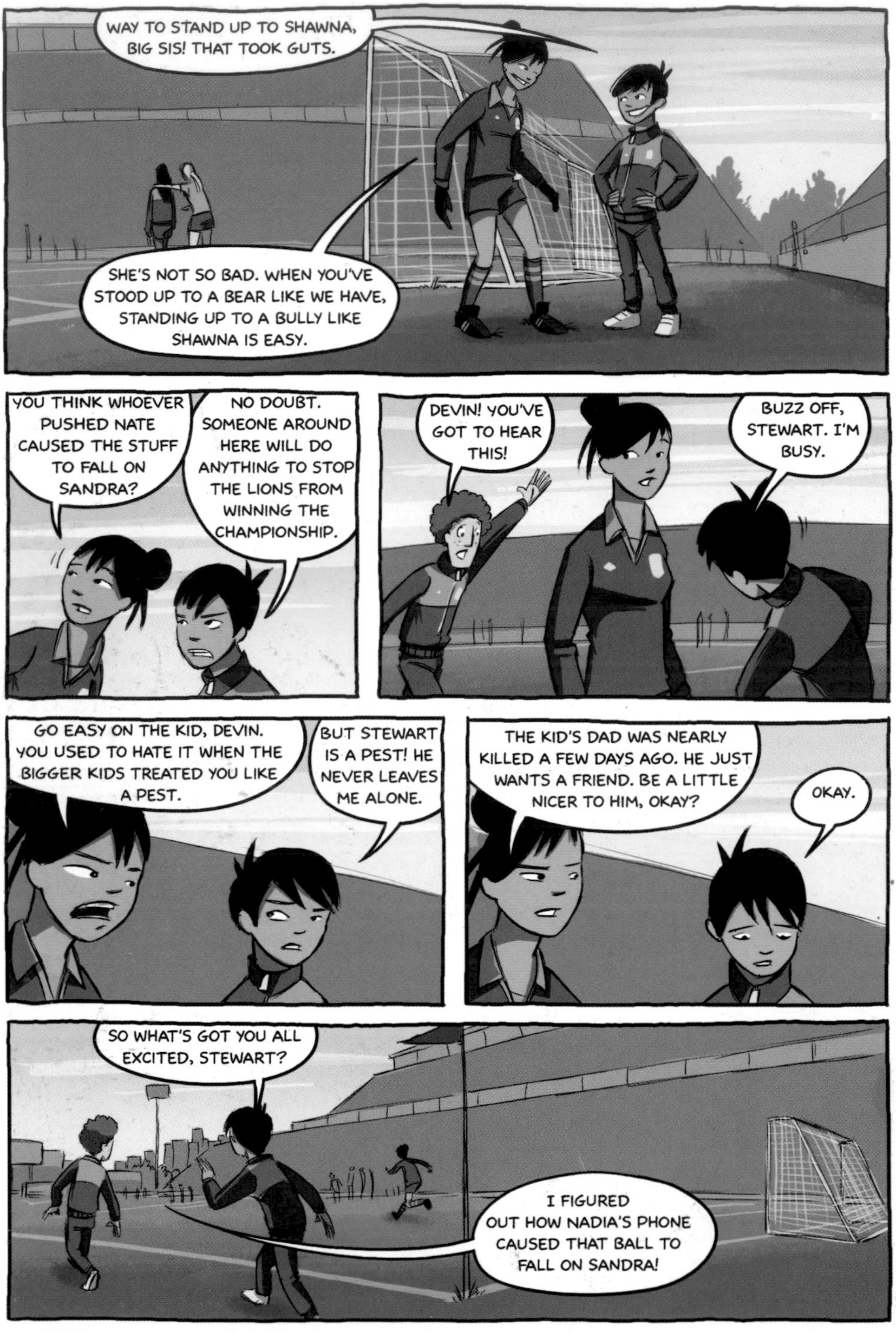
WAY TO STAND UP TO SHAWNA, BIG SIS! THAT TOOK GUTS.
SHE'S NOT SO BAD. WHEN YOU'VE STOOD UP TO A BEAR LIKE WE HAVE, STANDING UP TO A BULLY LIKE SHAWNA IS EASY.
YOU THINK WHOEVER PUSHED NATE CAUSED THE STUFF TO FALL ON SANDRA?
NO DOUBT. SOMEONE AROUND HERE WILL DO ANYTHING TO STOP THE LIONS FROM WINNING THE CHAMPIONSHIP.
DEVIN! YOU'VE GOT TO HEAR THIS!
BUZZ OFF, STEWART. I'M BUSY.
GO EASY ON THE KID, DEVIN. YOU USED TO HATE IT WHEN THE BIGGER KIDS TREATED YOU LIKE A PEST.
BUT STEWART IS A PEST! HE NEVER LEAVES ME ALONE.
THE KID'S DAD WAS NEARLY KILLED A FEW DAYS AGO. HE JUST WANTS A FRIEND. BE A LITTLE NICER TO HIM, OKAY?
OKAY.
SO WHAT'S GOT YOU ALL EXCITED, STEWART?
I FIGURED OUT HOW NADIA'S PHONE CAUSED THAT BALL TO FALL ON SANDRA!

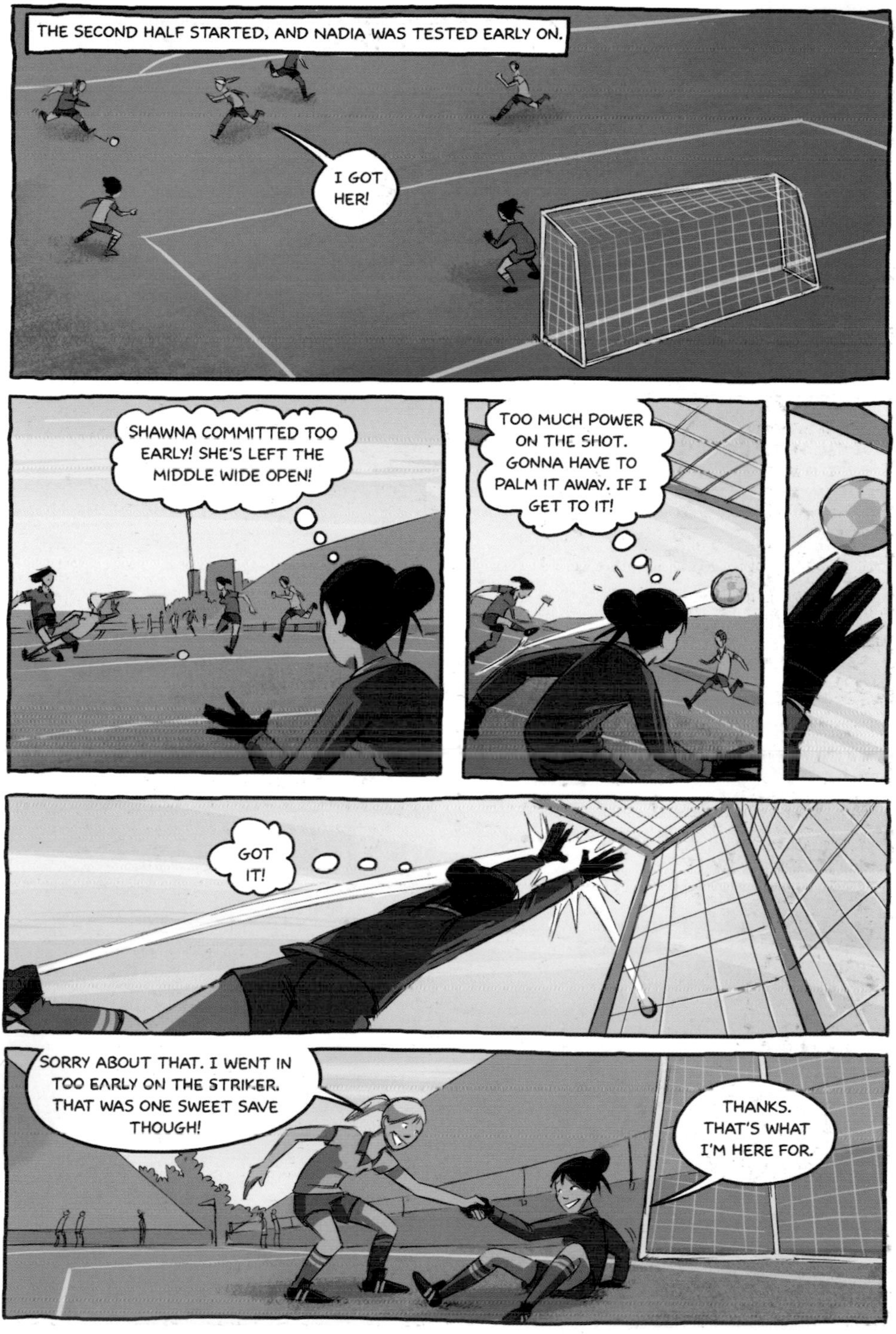
THE SECOND HALF STARTED, AND NADIA WAS TESTED EARLY ON.
I GOT HER!
SHAWNA COMMITTED TOO EARLY! SHE'S LEFT THE MIDDLE WIDE OPEN!
TOO MUCH POWER ON THE SHOT. GONNA HAVE TO PALM IT AWAY. IF I GET TO IT!
GOT IT!
SORRY ABOUT THAT. I WENT IN TOO EARLY ON THE STRIKER. THAT WAS ONE SWEET SAVE THOUGH!
THANKS. THAT'S WHAT I'M HERE FOR.

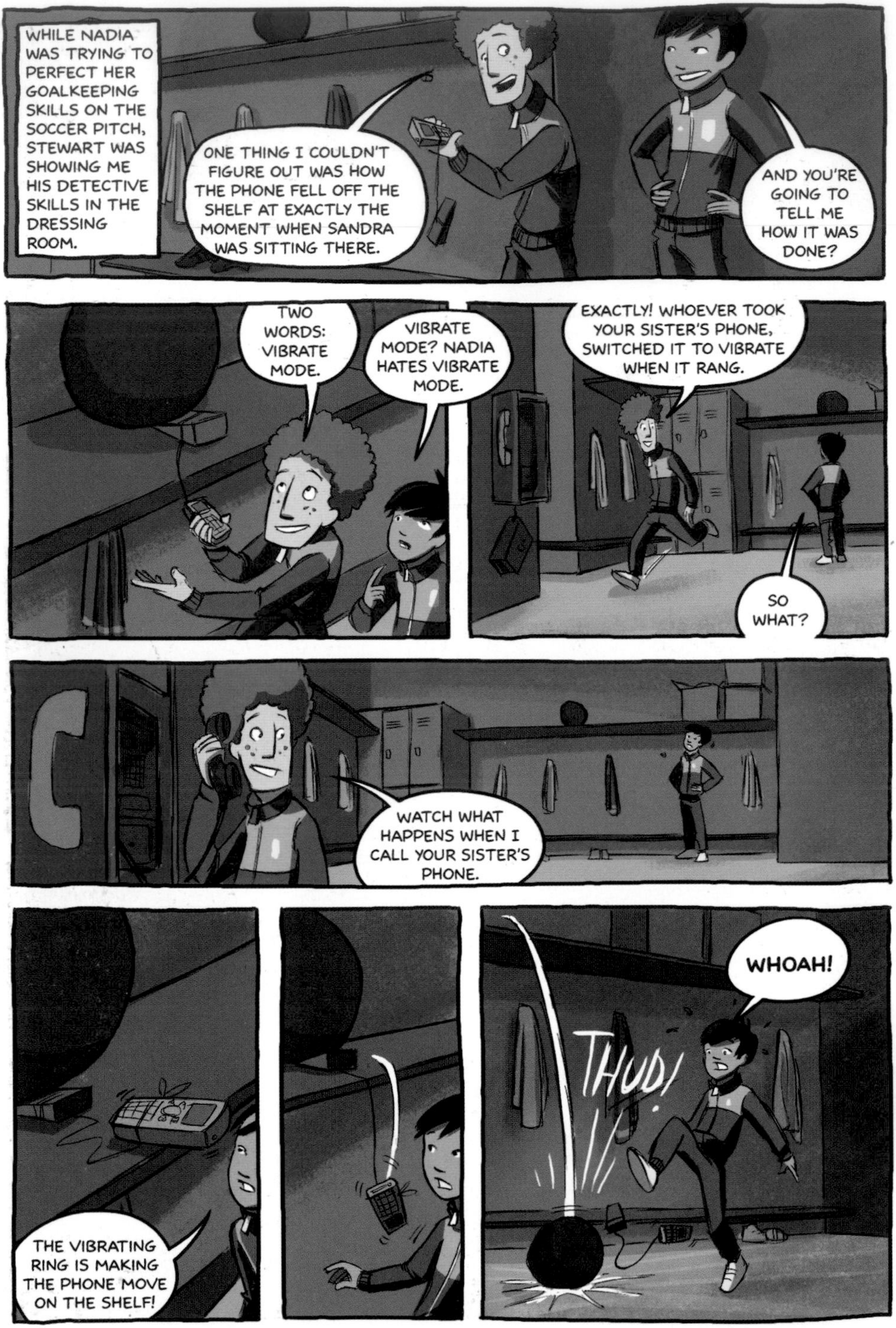

WHILE NADIA WAS TRYING TO PERFECT HER GOALKEEPING SKILLS ON THE SOCCER PITCH, STEWART WAS SHOWING ME HIS DETECTIVE SKILLS IN THE DRESSING ROOM.
ONE THING I COULDN'T FIGURE OUT WAS HOW THE PHONE FELL OFF THE SHELF AT EXACTLY THE MOMENT WHEN SANDRA WAS SITTING THERE.
AND YOU'RE GOING TO TELL ME HOW IT WAS DONE?
TWO WORDS: VIBRATE MODE.
VIBRATE MODE? NADIA HATES VIBRATE MODE.
EXACTLY! WHOEVER TOOK YOUR SISTER'S PHONE, SWITCHED IT TO VIBRATE WHEN IT RANG.
SO WHAT?
WATCH WHAT HAPPENS WHEN I CALL YOUR SISTER'S PHONE.
THE VIBRATING RING IS MAKING THE PHONE MOVE ON THE SHELF!
WHOAH!
THUD!

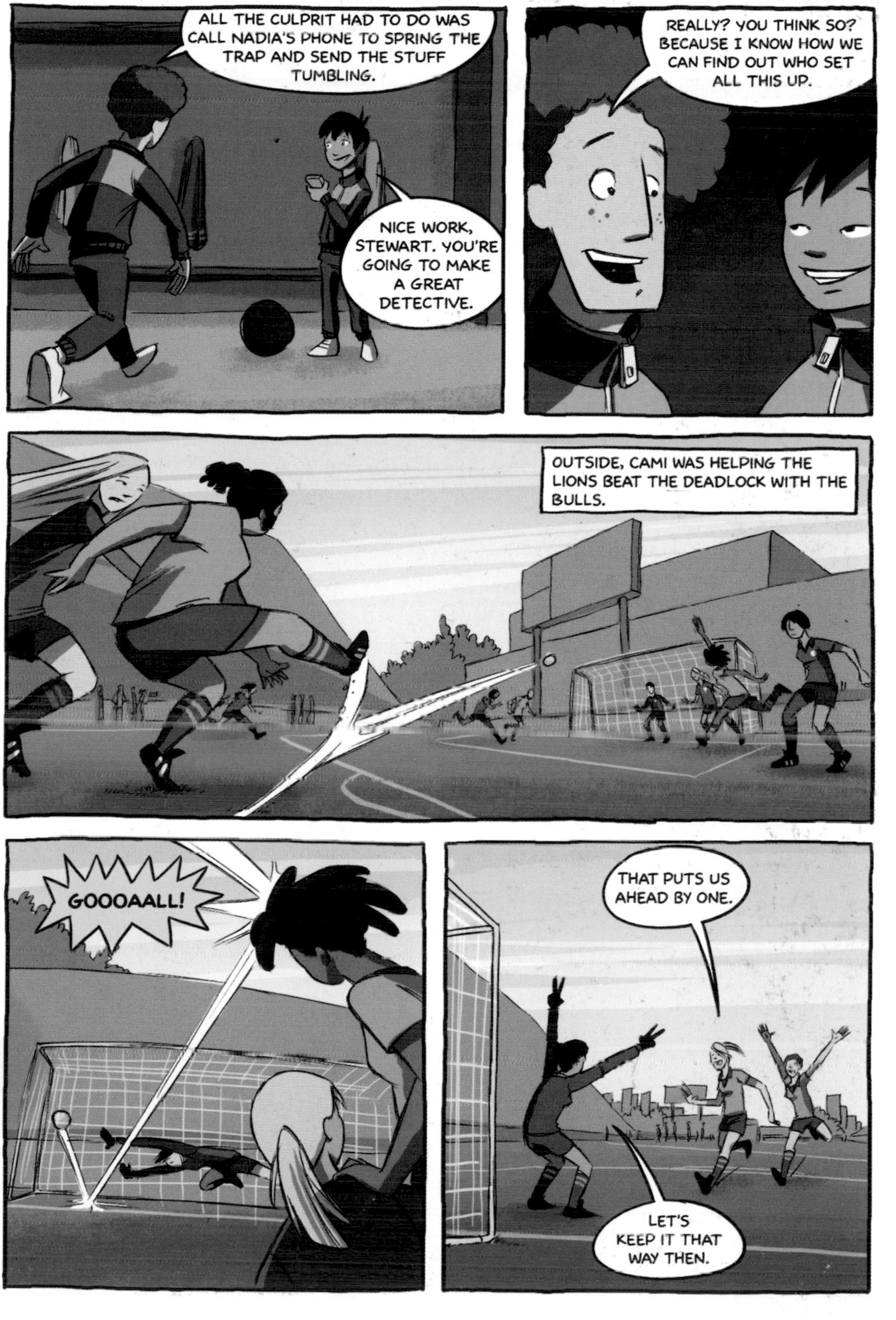
ALL THE CULPRIT HAD TO DO WAS CALL NADIA'S PHONE TO SPRING THE TRAP AND SEND THE STUFF TUMBLING.
NICE WORK, STEWART. YOU'RE GOING TO MAKE A GREAT DETECTIVE.
REALLY? YOU THINK SO? BECAUSE I KNOW HOW WE CAN FIND OUT WHO SET ALL THIS UP.
OUTSIDE, CAMI WAS HELPING THE LIONS BEAT THE DEADLOCK WITH THE BULLS.
GOOOAALL!
THAT PUTS US AHEAD BY ONE.
LET'S KEEP IT THAT WAY THEN.

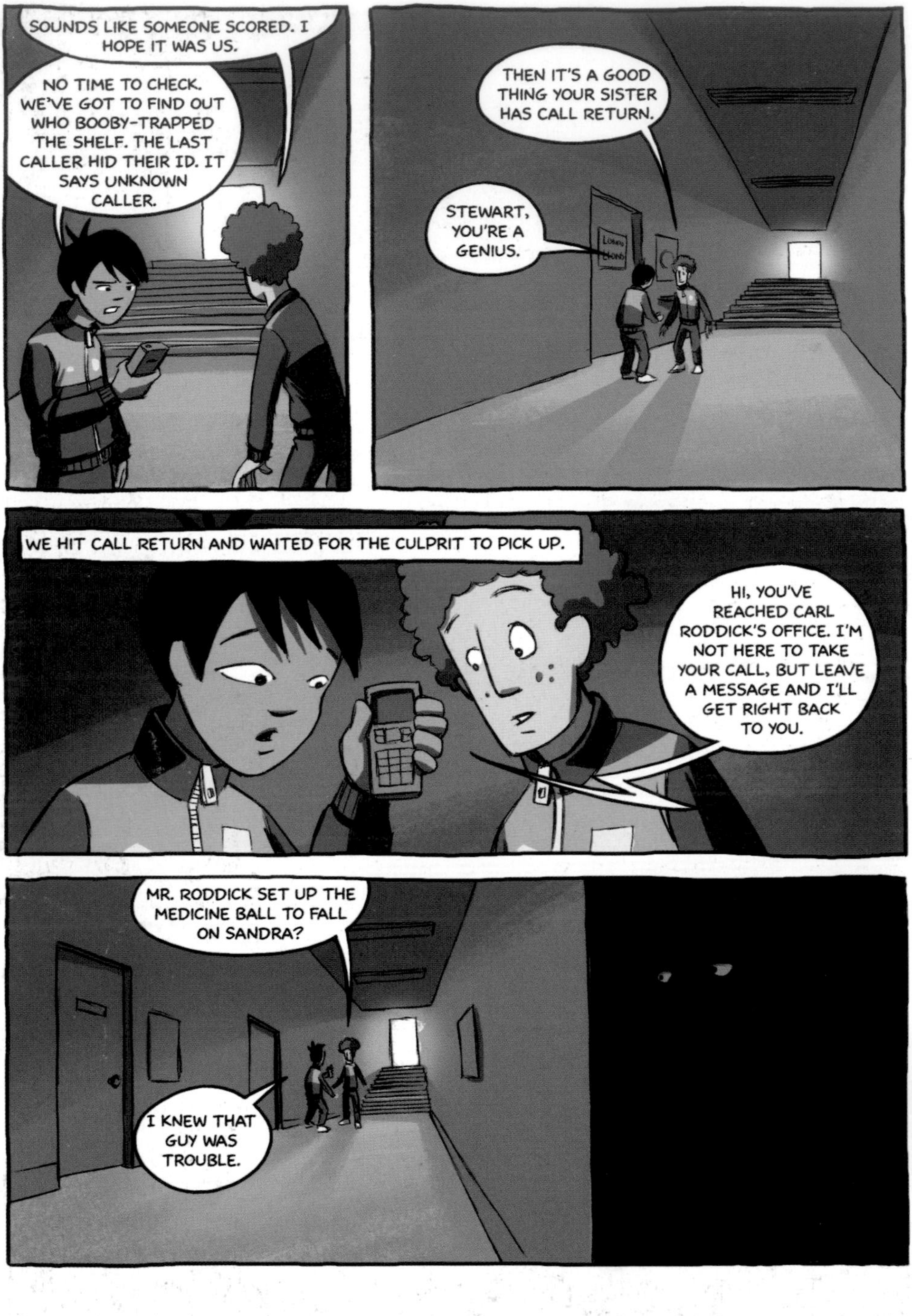
SOUNDS LIKE SOMEONE SCORED. I HOPE IT WAS US.
NO TIME TO CHECK. WE'VE GOT TO FIND OUT WHO BOOBY-TRAPPED THE SHELF. THE LAST CALLER HID THEIR ID. IT SAYS UNKNOWN CALLER.
THEN IT'S A GOOD THING YOUR SISTER HAS CALL RETURN.
STEWART, YOU'RE A GENIUS.
WE HIT CALL RETURN AND WAITED FOR THE CULPRIT TO PICK UP.
HI, YOU'VE REACHED CARL RODDICK'S OFFICE. I'M NOT HERE TO TAKE YOUR CALL, BUT LEAVE A MESSAGE AND I'LL GET RIGHT BACK TO YOU.
MR. RODDICK SET UP THE MEDICINE BALL TO FALL ON SANDRA?
I KNEW THAT GUY WAS TROUBLE.

CHAPTER 5
THE LIONS BITE BACK

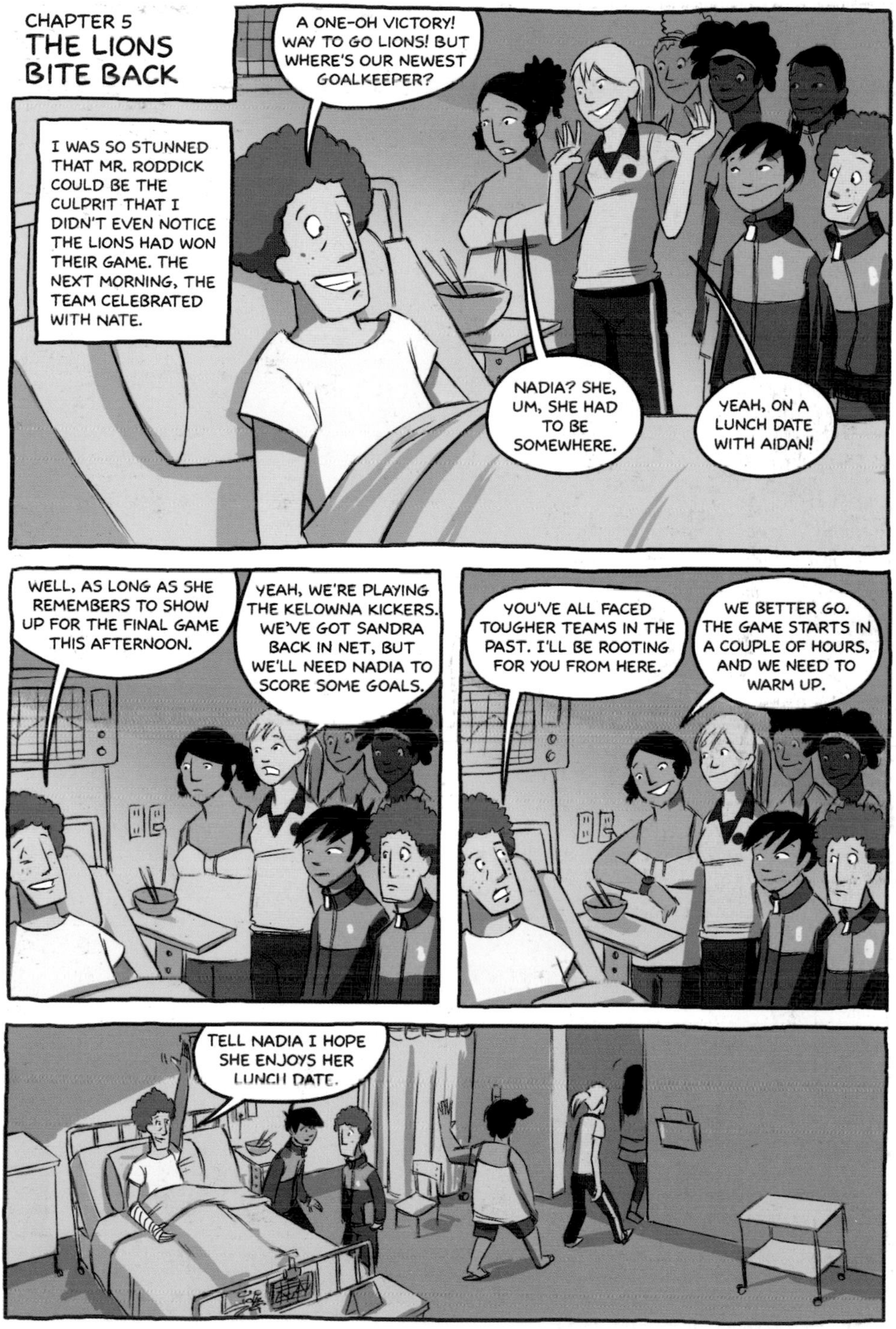

A ONE-OH VICTORY! WAY TO GO LIONS! BUT WHERE'S OUR NEWEST GOALKEEPER?
I WAS SO STUNNED THAT MR. RODDICK COULD BE THE CULPRIT THAT I DIDN'T EVEN NOTICE THE LIONS HAD WON THEIR GAME. THE NEXT MORNING, THE TEAM CELEBRATED WITH NATE.
NADIA? SHE, UM, SHE HAD TO BE SOMEWHERE.
YEAH, ON A LUNCH DATE WITH AIDAN!
WELL, AS LONG AS SHE REMEMBERS TO SHOW UP FOR THE FINAL GAME THIS AFTERNOON.
YEAH, WE'RE PLAYING THE KELOWNA KICKERS. WE'VE GOT SANDRA BACK IN NET, BUT WE'LL NEED NADIA TO SCORE SOME GOALS.
YOU'VE ALL FACED TOUGHER TEAMS IN THE PAST. I'LL BE ROOTING FOR YOU FROM HERE.
WE BETTER GO. THE GAME STARTS IN A COUPLE OF HOURS, AND WE NEED TO WARM UP.
TELL NADIA I HOPE SHE ENJOYS HER LUNCH DATE.

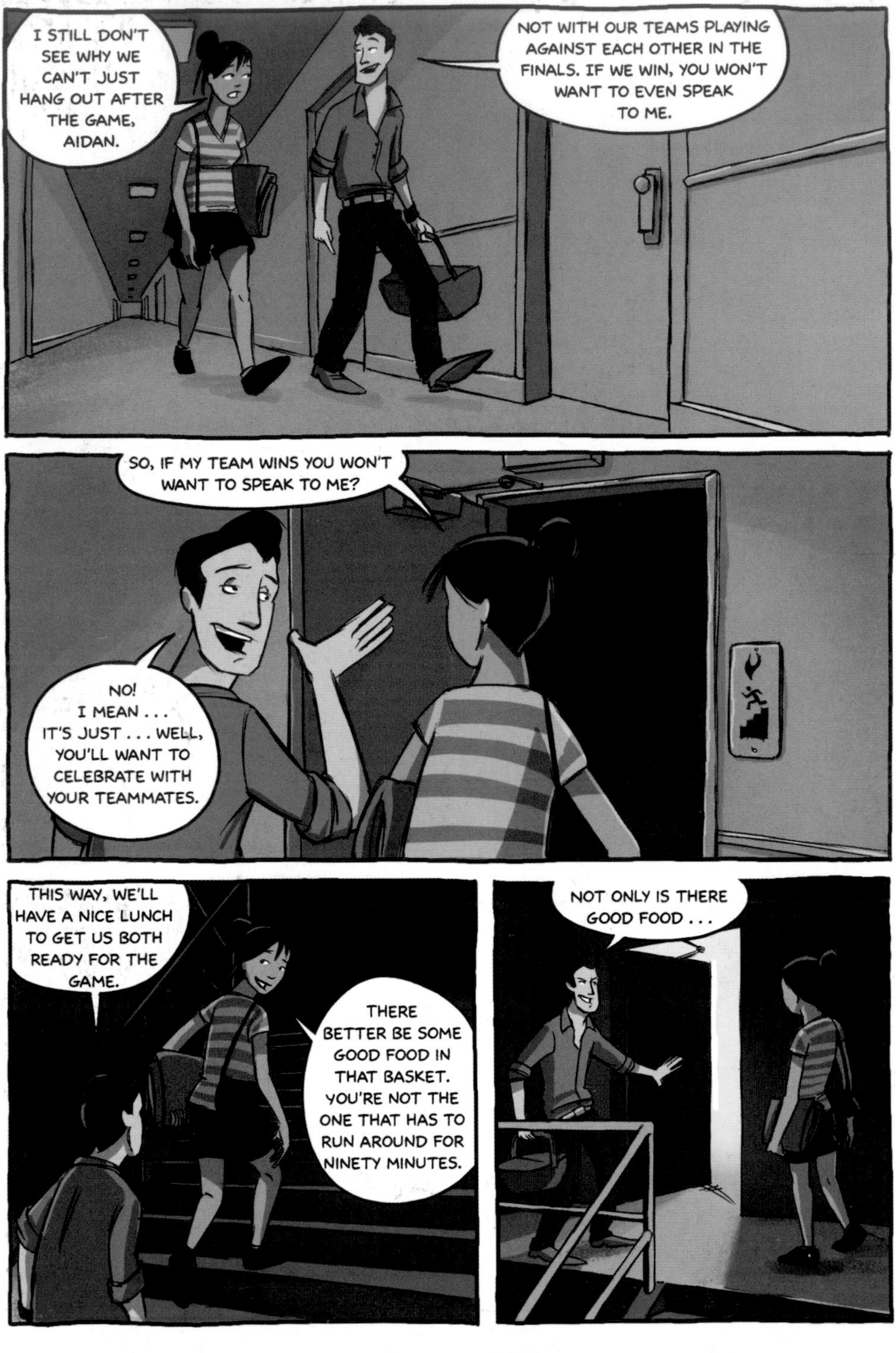
I STILL DON'T SEE WHY WE CAN'T JUST HANG OUT AFTER THE GAME, AIDAN.
NOT WITH OUR TEAMS PLAYING AGAINST EACH OTHER IN THE FINALS. IF WE WIN, YOU WON'T WANT TO EVEN SPEAK TO ME.
SO, IF MY TEAM WINS YOU WON'T WANT TO SPEAK TO ME?
NO! I MEAN . . . IT'S JUST . . . WELL, YOU'LL WANT TO CELEBRATE WITH YOUR TEAMMATES.
THIS WAY, WE'LL HAVE A NICE LUNCH TO GET US BOTH READY FOR THE GAME.
THERE BETTER BE SOME GOOD FOOD IN THAT BASKET. YOU'RE NOT THE ONE THAT HAS TO RUN AROUND FOR NINETY MINUTES.
NOT ONLY IS THERE GOOD FOOD . . .

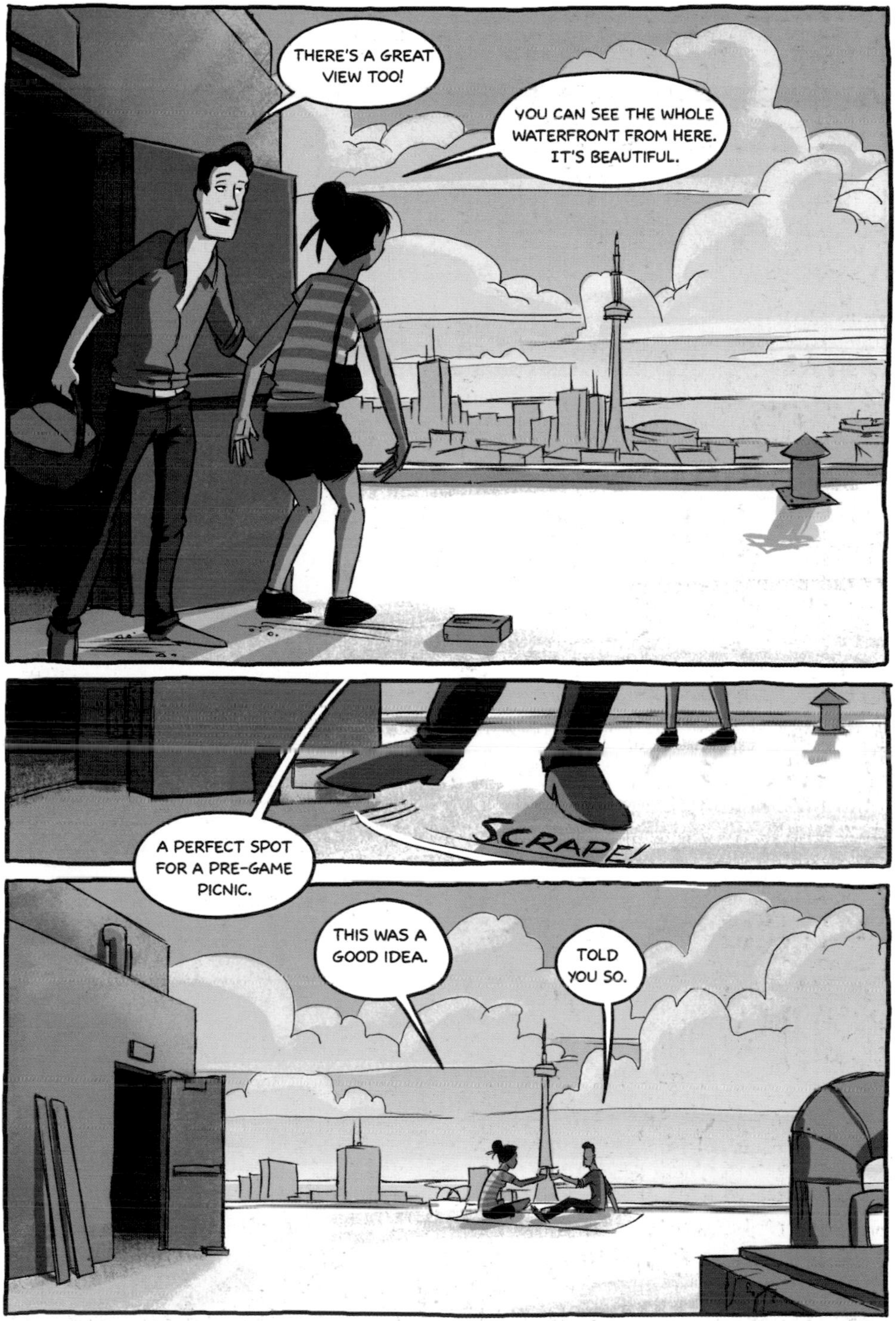
THERE'S A GREAT VIEW TOO!
YOU CAN SEE THE WHOLE WATERFRONT FROM HERE. IT'S BEAUTIFUL.
SCRAPE!
A PERFECT SPOT FOR A PRE-GAME PICNIC.
THIS WAS A GOOD IDEA.
TOLD YOU SO.

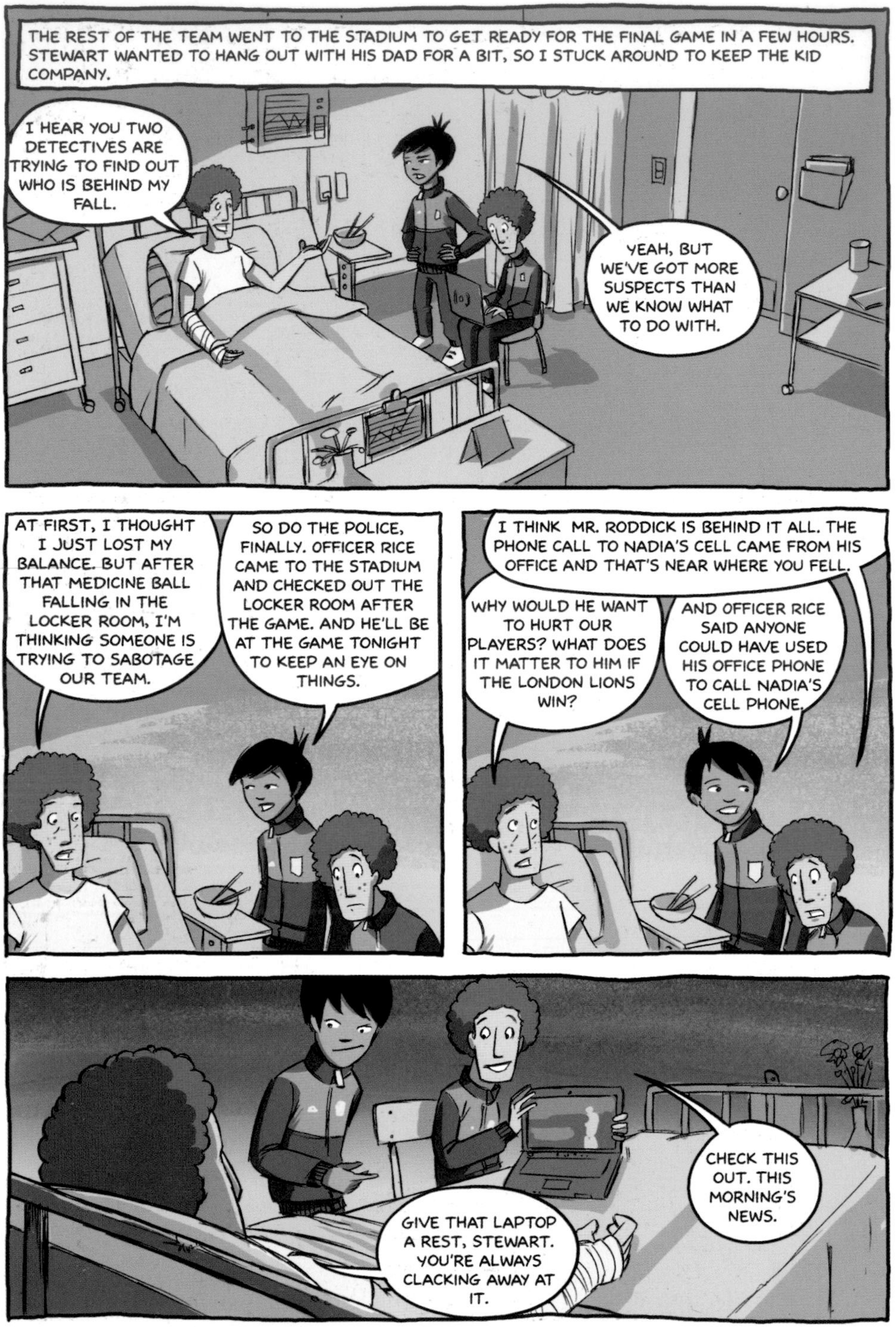
THE REST OF THE TEAM WENT TO THE STADIUM TO GET READY FOR THE FINAL GAME IN A FEW HOURS. STEWART WANTED TO HANG OUT WITH HIS DAD FOR A BIT, SO I STUCK AROUND TO KEEP THE KID COMPANY.
I HEAR YOU TWO DETECTIVES ARE TRYING TO FIND OUT WHO IS BEHIND MY FALL.
YEAH, BUT WE'VE GOT MORE SUSPECTS THAN WE KNOW WHAT TO DO WITH.
AT FIRST, I THOUGHT I JUST LOST MY BALANCE. BUT AFTER THAT MEDICINE BALL FALLING IN THE LOCKER ROOM, I'M THINKING SOMEONE IS TRYING TO SABOTAGE OUR TEAM.
SO DO THE POLICE, FINALLY. OFFICER RICE CAME TO THE STADIUM AND CHECKED OUT THE LOCKER ROOM AFTER THE GAME. AND HE'LL BE AT THE GAME TONIGHT TO KEEP AN EYE ON THINGS.
I THINK MR. RODDICK IS BEHIND IT ALL. THE PHONE CALL TO NADIA'S CELL CAME FROM HIS OFFICE AND THAT'S NEAR WHERE YOU FELL.
WHY WOULD HE WANT TO HURT OUR PLAYERS? WHAT DOES IT MATTER TO HIM IF THE LONDON LIONS WIN?
AND OFFICER RICE SAID ANYONE COULD HAVE USED HIS OFFICE PHONE TO CALL NADIA'S CELL PHONE.
GIVE THAT LAPTOP A REST, STEWART. YOU'RE ALWAYS CLACKING AWAY AT IT.
CHECK THIS OUT. THIS MORNING'S NEWS.

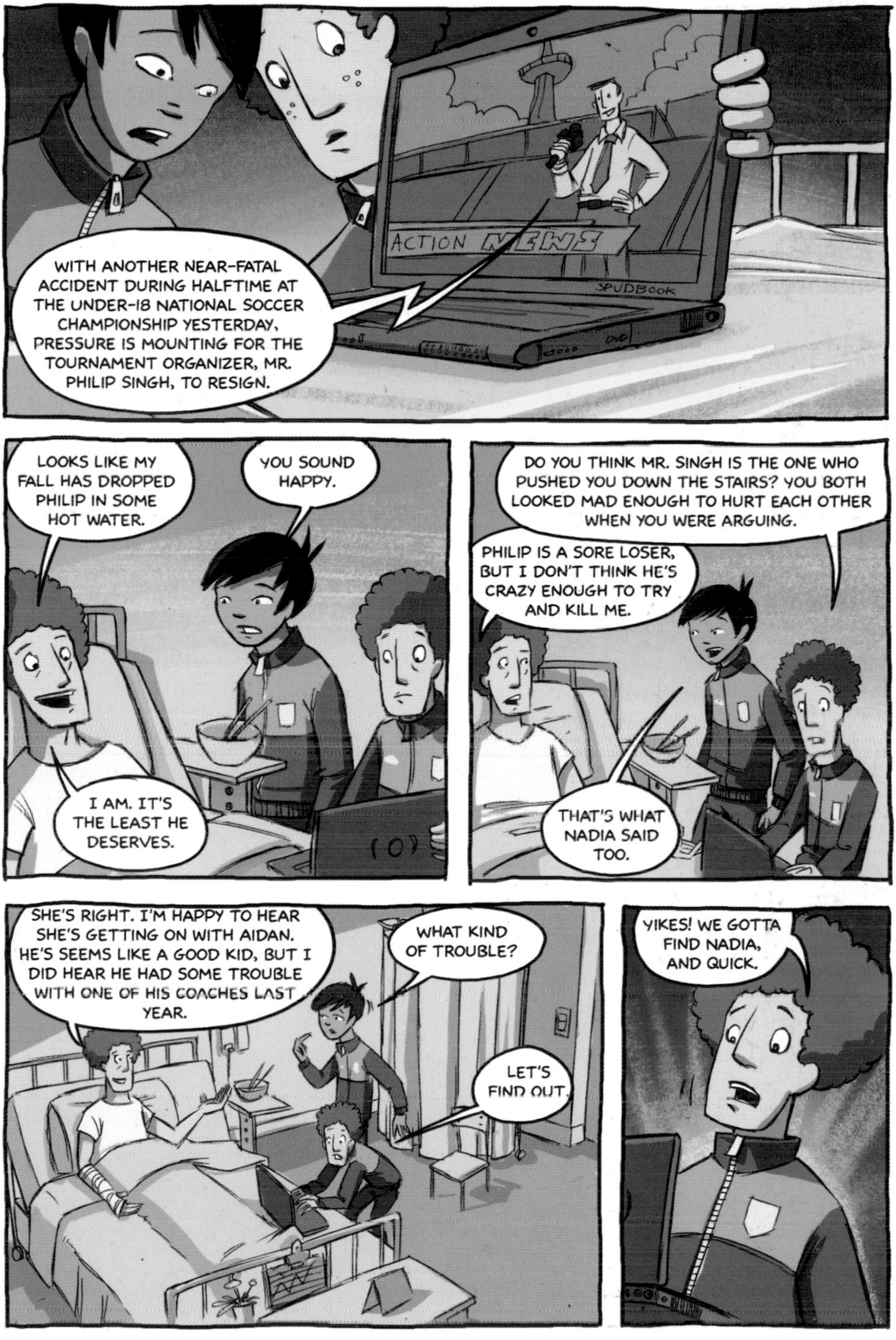
ACTION NEWS
SPUDBook
WITH ANOTHER NEAR-FATAL ACCIDENT DURING HALFTIME AT THE UNDER-18 NATIONAL SOCCER CHAMPIONSHIP YESTERDAY, PRESSURE IS MOUNTING FOR THE TOURNAMENT ORGANIZER, MR. PHILIP SINGH, TO RESIGN.
LOOKS LIKE MY FALL HAS DROPPED PHILIP IN SOME HOT WATER.
YOU SOUND HAPPY.
I AM. IT'S THE LEAST HE DESERVES.
DO YOU THINK MR. SINGH IS THE ONE WHO PUSHED YOU DOWN THE STAIRS? YOU BOTH LOOKED MAD ENOUGH TO HURT EACH OTHER WHEN YOU WERE ARGUING.
PHILIP IS A SORE LOSER, BUT I DON'T THINK HE'S CRAZY ENOUGH TO TRY AND KILL ME.
THAT'S WHAT NADIA SAID TOO.
SHE'S RIGHT. I'M HAPPY TO HEAR SHE'S GETTING ON WITH AIDAN. HE'S SEEMS LIKE A GOOD KID, BUT I DID HEAR HE HAD SOME TROUBLE WITH ONE OF HIS COACHES LAST YEAR.
WHAT KIND OF TROUBLE?
LET'S FIND OUT.
YIKES! WE GOTTA FIND NADIA, AND QUICK.

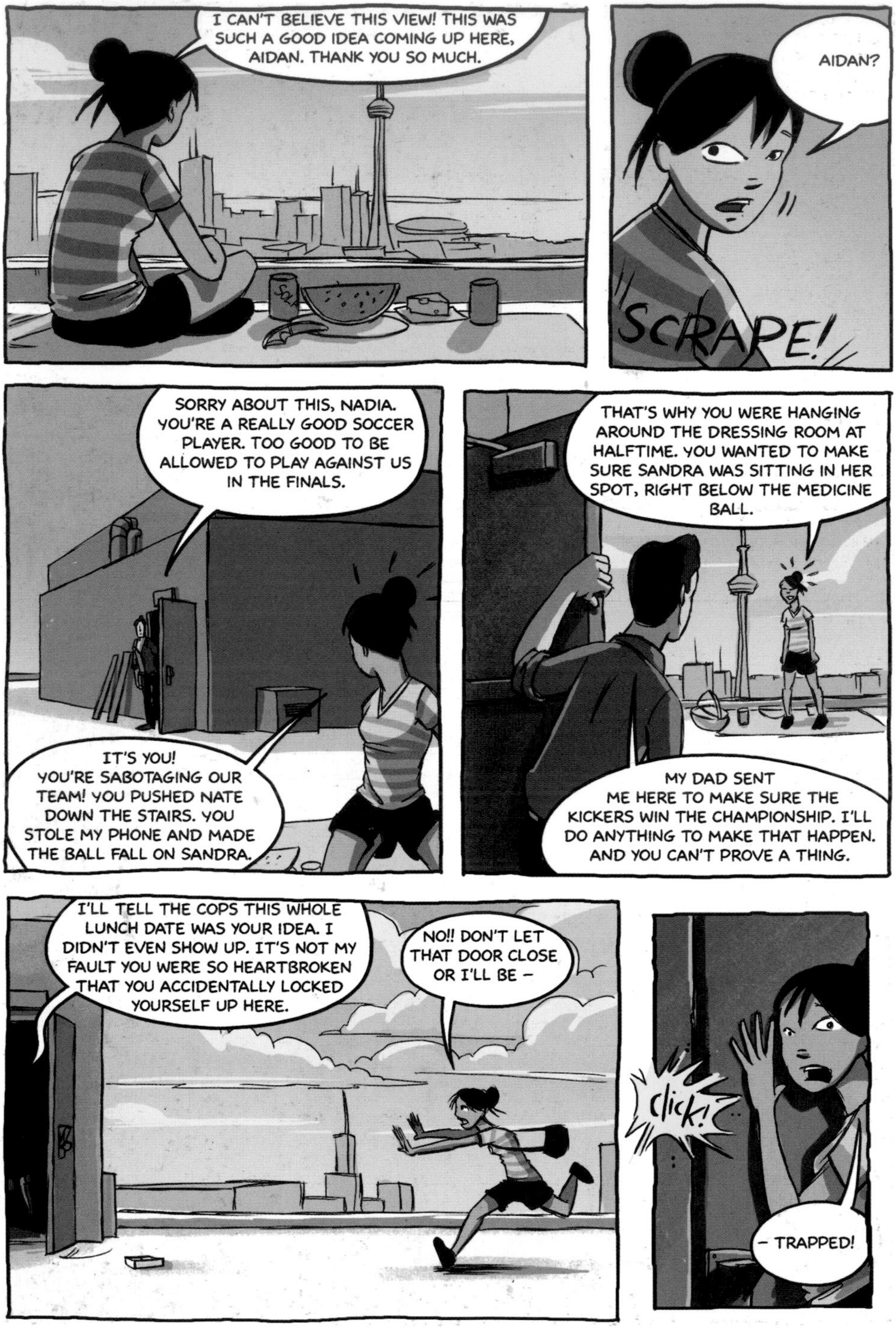
I CAN'T BELIEVE THIS VIEW! THIS WAS SUCH A GOOD IDEA COMING UP HERE, AIDAN. THANK YOU SO MUCH.
AIDAN?
SCRAPE!
SORRY ABOUT THIS, NADIA. YOU'RE A REALLY GOOD SOCCER PLAYER. TOO GOOD TO BE ALLOWED TO PLAY AGAINST US IN THE FINALS.
IT'S YOU! YOU'RE SABOTAGING OUR TEAM! YOU PUSHED NATE DOWN THE STAIRS. YOU STOLE MY PHONE AND MADE THE BALL FALL ON SANDRA.
THAT'S WHY YOU WERE HANGING AROUND THE DRESSING ROOM AT HALFTIME. YOU WANTED TO MAKE SURE SANDRA WAS SITTING IN HER SPOT, RIGHT BELOW THE MEDICINE BALL.
MY DAD SENT ME HERE TO MAKE SURE THE KICKERS WIN THE CHAMPIONSHIP. I'LL DO ANYTHING TO MAKE THAT HAPPEN. AND YOU CAN'T PROVE A THING.
I'LL TELL THE COPS THIS WHOLE LUNCH DATE WAS YOUR IDEA. I DIDN'T EVEN SHOW UP. IT'S NOT MY FAULT YOU WERE SO HEARTBROKEN THAT YOU ACCIDENTALLY LOCKED YOURSELF UP HERE.
NO!! DON'T LET THAT DOOR CLOSE OR I'LL BE –
click!
– TRAPPED!

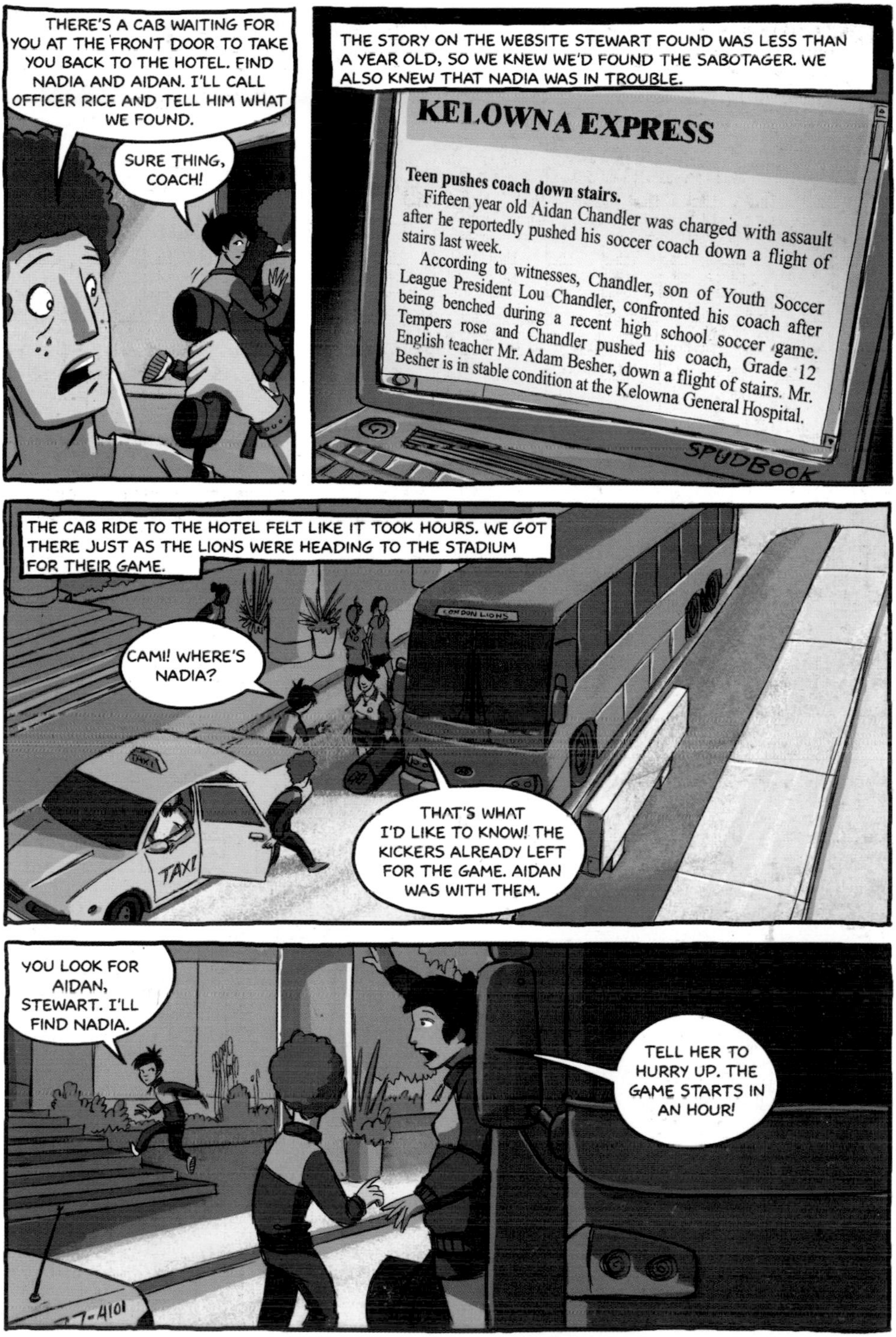

THERE'S A CAB WAITING FOR YOU AT THE FRONT DOOR TO TAKE YOU BACK TO THE HOTEL. FIND NADIA AND AIDAN. I'LL CALL OFFICER RICE AND TELL HIM WHAT WE FOUND.
SURE THING, COACH!
THE STORY ON THE WEBSITE STEWART FOUND WAS LESS THAN A YEAR OLD, SO WE KNEW WE'D FOUND THE SABOTAGER. WE ALSO KNEW THAT NADIA WAS IN TROUBLE.
KELOWNA EXPRESS
Teen pushes coach down stairs.
Fifteen year old Aidan Chandler was charged with assault after he reportedly pushed his soccer coach down a flight of stairs last week.
According to witnesses, Chandler, son of Youth Soccer League President Lou Chandler, confronted his coach after being benched during a recent high school soccer game. Tempers rose and Chandler pushed his coach, Grade 12 English teacher Mr. Adam Besher, down a flight of stairs. Mr. Besher is in stable condition at the Kelowna General Hospital.
SPUDBOOK
THE CAB RIDE TO THE HOTEL FELT LIKE IT TOOK HOURS. WE GOT THERE JUST AS THE LIONS WERE HEADING TO THE STADIUM FOR THEIR GAME.
LONDON LIONS
CAMI! WHERE'S NADIA?
TAXI
TAXI
THAT'S WHAT I'D LIKE TO KNOW! THE KICKERS ALREADY LEFT FOR THE GAME. AIDAN WAS WITH THEM.
YOU LOOK FOR AIDAN, STEWART. I'LL FIND NADIA.
TELL HER TO HURRY UP. THE GAME STARTS IN AN HOUR!

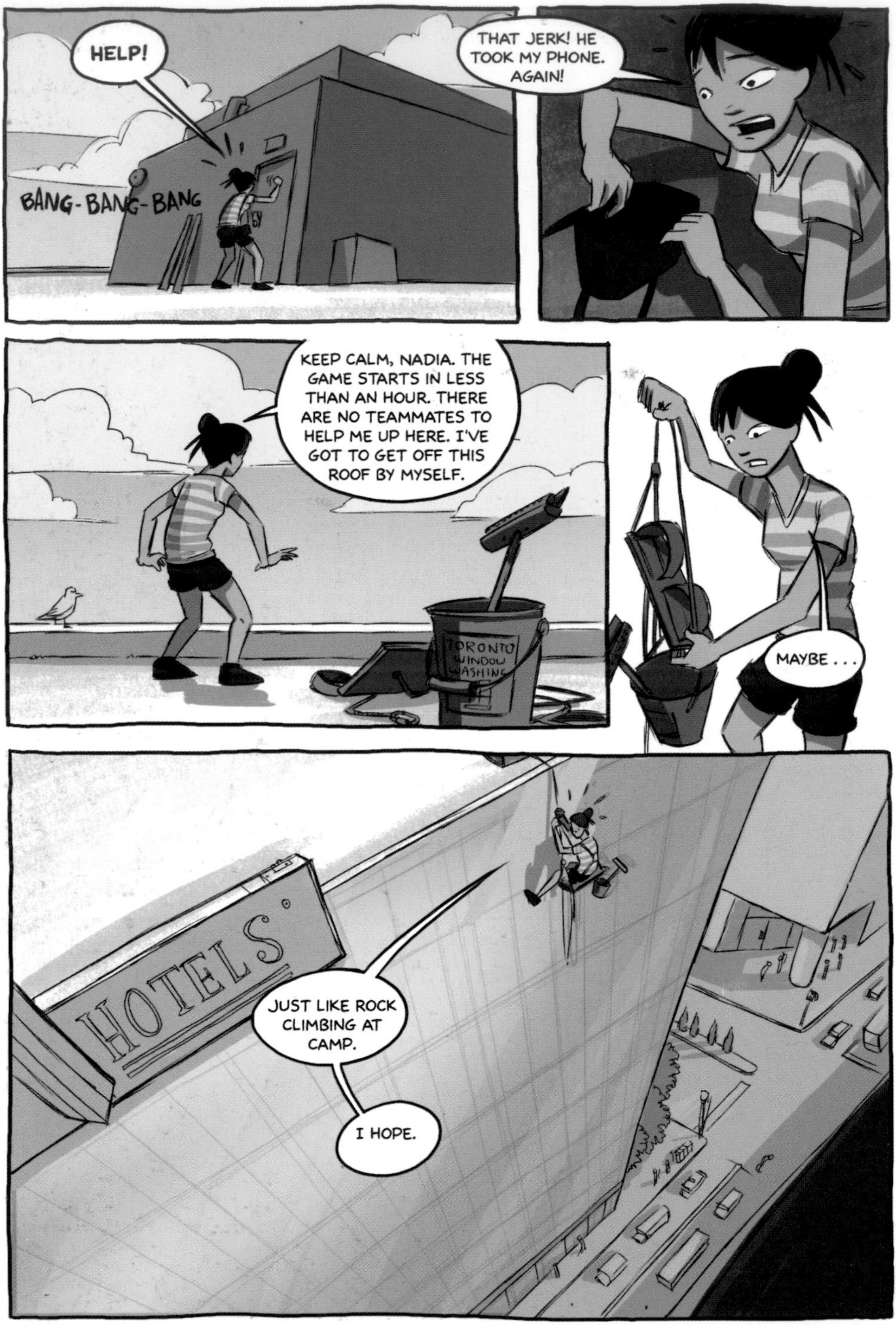
HELP!
BANG-BANG-BANG
THAT JERK! HE TOOK MY PHONE. AGAIN!
KEEP CALM, NADIA. THE GAME STARTS IN LESS THAN AN HOUR. THERE ARE NO TEAMMATES TO HELP ME UP HERE. I'VE GOT TO GET OFF THIS ROOF BY MYSELF.
TORONTO WINDOW WASHING
MAYBE . . .
HOTELS
JUST LIKE ROCK CLIMBING AT CAMP.
I HOPE.

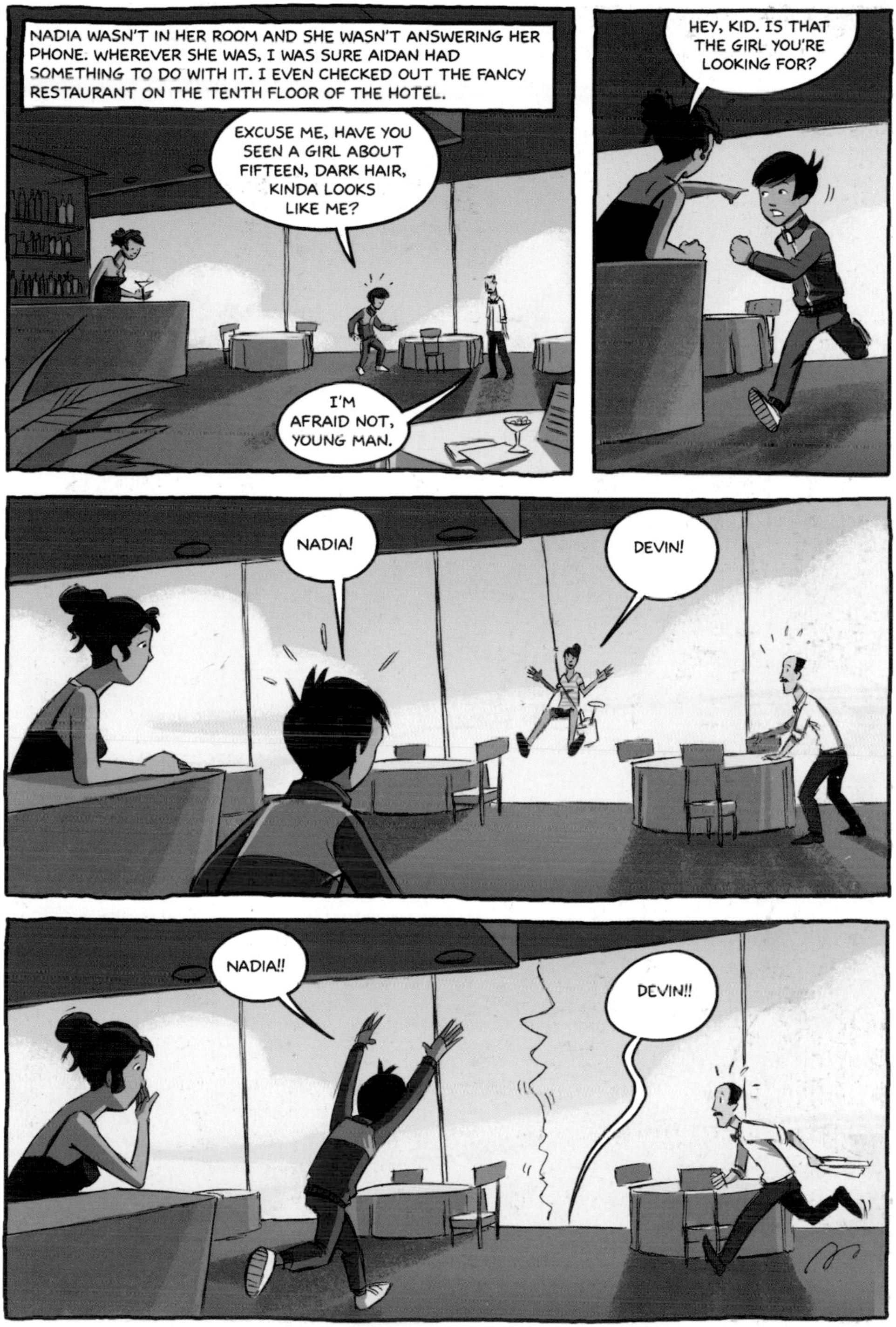
NADIA WASN'T IN HER ROOM AND SHE WASN'T ANSWERING HER PHONE. WHEREVER SHE WAS, I WAS SURE AIDAN HAD SOMETHING TO DO WITH IT. I EVEN CHECKED OUT THE FANCY RESTAURANT ON THE TENTH FLOOR OF THE HOTEL.
EXCUSE ME, HAVE YOU SEEN A GIRL ABOUT FIFTEEN, DARK HAIR, KINDA LOOKS LIKE ME?
I'M AFRAID NOT, YOUNG MAN.
HEY, KID. IS THAT THE GIRL YOU'RE LOOKING FOR?
NADIA!
DEVIN!
NADIA!!
DEVIN!!

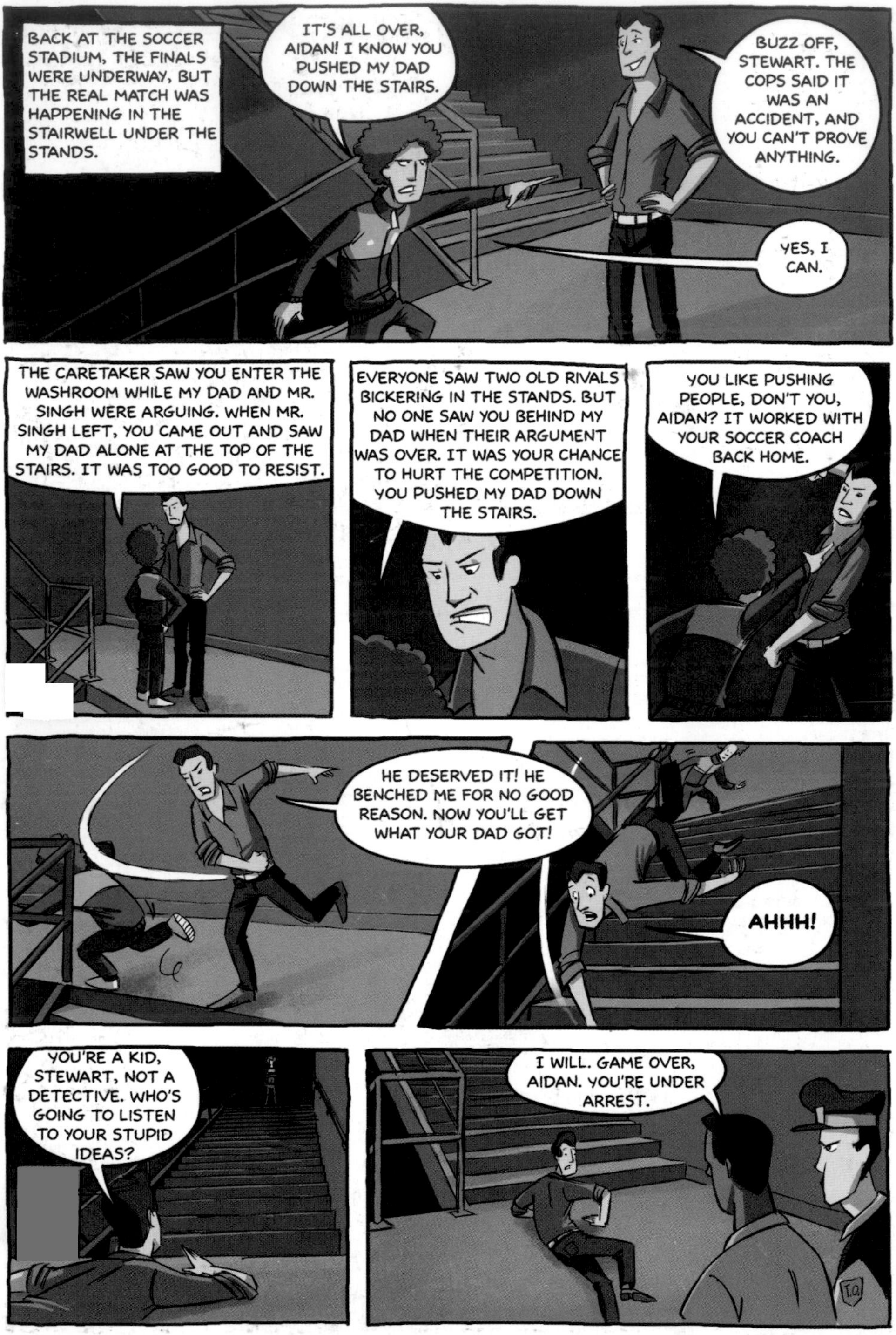

BACK AT THE SOCCER STADIUM, THE FINALS WERE UNDERWAY, BUT THE REAL MATCH WAS HAPPENING IN THE STAIRWELL UNDER THE STANDS.
IT'S ALL OVER, AIDAN! I KNOW YOU PUSHED MY DAD DOWN THE STAIRS.
BUZZ OFF, STEWART. THE COPS SAID IT WAS AN ACCIDENT, AND YOU CAN'T PROVE ANYTHING.
YES, I CAN.
THE CARETAKER SAW YOU ENTER THE WASHROOM WHILE MY DAD AND MR. SINGH WERE ARGUING. WHEN MR. SINGH LEFT, YOU CAME OUT AND SAW MY DAD ALONE AT THE TOP OF THE STAIRS. IT WAS TOO GOOD TO RESIST.
EVERYONE SAW TWO OLD RIVALS BICKERING IN THE STANDS. BUT NO ONE SAW YOU BEHIND MY DAD WHEN THEIR ARGUMENT WAS OVER. IT WAS YOUR CHANCE TO HURT THE COMPETITION. YOU PUSHED MY DAD DOWN THE STAIRS.
YOU LIKE PUSHING PEOPLE, DON'T YOU, AIDAN? IT WORKED WITH YOUR SOCCER COACH BACK HOME.
HE DESERVED IT! HE BENCHED ME FOR NO GOOD REASON. NOW YOU'LL GET WHAT YOUR DAD GOT!
AHHH!
YOU'RE A KID, STEWART, NOT A DETECTIVE. WHO'S GOING TO LISTEN TO YOUR STUPID IDEAS?
I WILL. GAME OVER, AIDAN. YOU'RE UNDER ARREST.

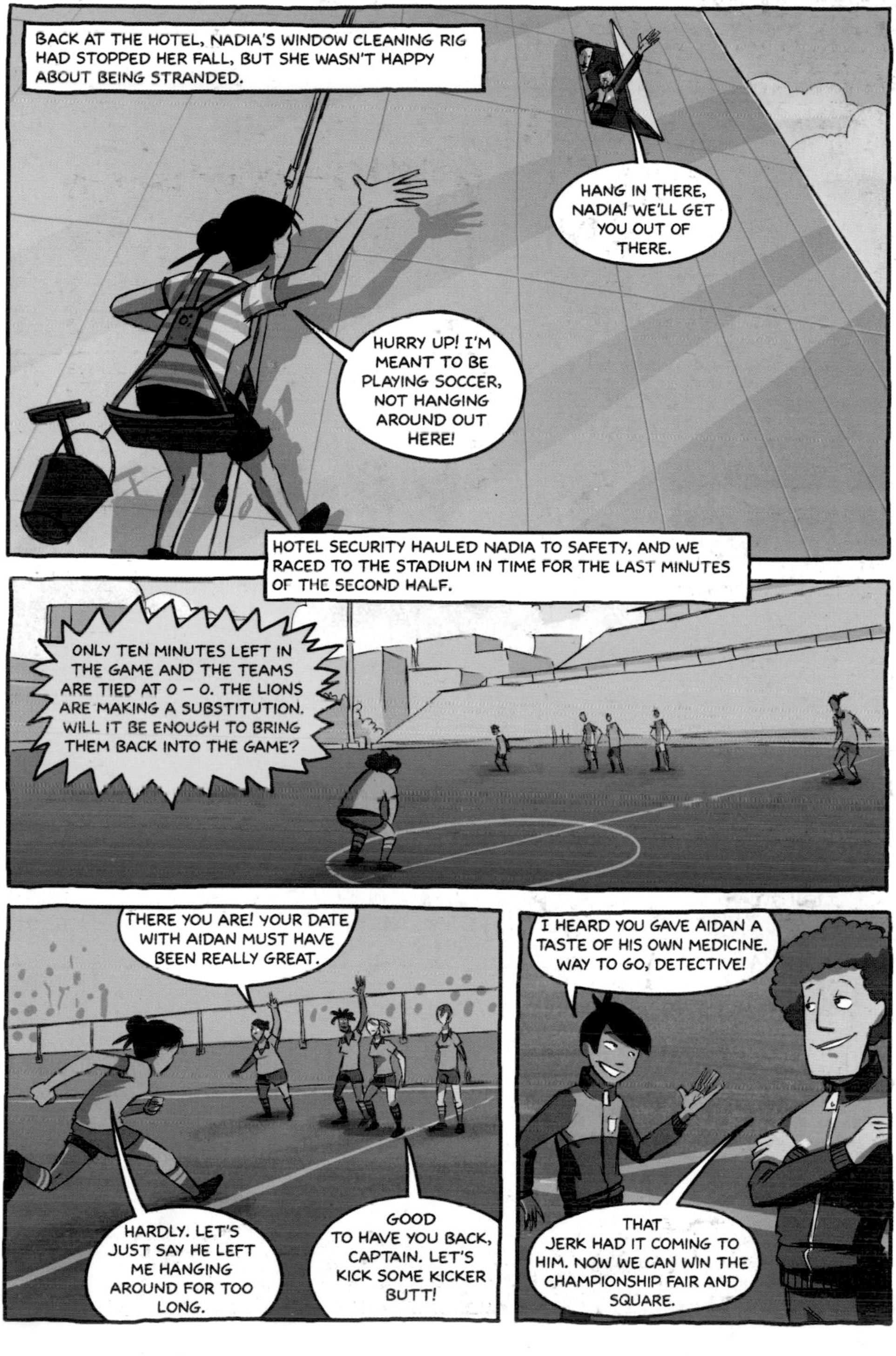
BACK AT THE HOTEL, NADIA'S WINDOW CLEANING RIG HAD STOPPED HER FALL, BUT SHE WASN'T HAPPY ABOUT BEING STRANDED.
HANG IN THERE, NADIA! WE'LL GET YOU OUT OF THERE.
HURRY UP! I'M MEANT TO BE PLAYING SOCCER, NOT HANGING AROUND OUT HERE!
HOTEL SECURITY HAULED NADIA TO SAFETY, AND WE RACED TO THE STADIUM IN TIME FOR THE LAST MINUTES OF THE SECOND HALF.
ONLY TEN MINUTES LEFT IN THE GAME AND THE TEAMS ARE TIED AT 0 – 0. THE LIONS ARE MAKING A SUBSTITUTION. WILL IT BE ENOUGH TO BRING THEM BACK INTO THE GAME?
THERE YOU ARE! YOUR DATE WITH AIDAN MUST HAVE BEEN REALLY GREAT.
HARDLY. LET'S JUST SAY HE LEFT ME HANGING AROUND FOR TOO LONG.
GOOD TO HAVE YOU BACK, CAPTAIN. LET'S KICK SOME KICKER BUTT!
I HEARD YOU GAVE AIDAN A TASTE OF HIS OWN MEDICINE. WAY TO GO, DETECTIVE!
THAT JERK HAD IT COMING TO HIM. NOW WE CAN WIN THE CHAMPIONSHIP FAIR AND SQUARE.

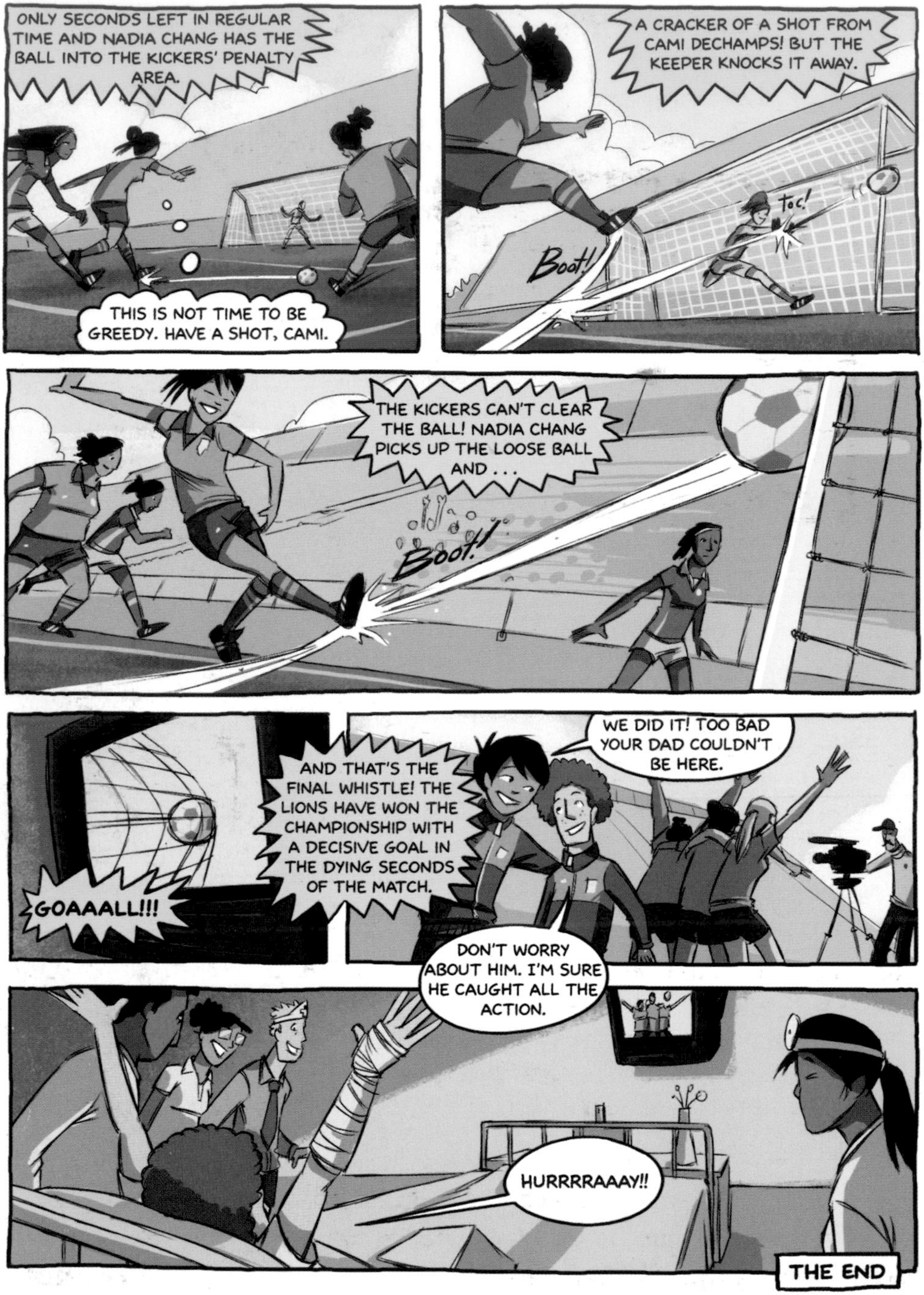
ONLY SECONDS LEFT IN REGULAR TIME AND NADIA CHANG HAS THE BALL INTO THE KICKERS' PENALTY AREA.
THIS IS NOT TIME TO BE GREEDY. HAVE A SHOT, CAMI.
A CRACKER OF A SHOT FROM CAMI DECHAMPS! BUT THE KEEPER KNOCKS IT AWAY.
Boot!
Toc!
THE KICKERS CAN'T CLEAR THE BALL! NADIA CHANG PICKS UP THE LOOSE BALL AND . . .
Boot!
GOAAALL!!!
AND THAT'S THE FINAL WHISTLE! THE LIONS HAVE WON THE CHAMPIONSHIP WITH A DECISIVE GOAL IN THE DYING SECONDS OF THE MATCH.
WE DID IT! TOO BAD YOUR DAD COULDN'T BE HERE.
DON'T WORRY ABOUT HIM. I'M SURE HE CAUGHT ALL THE ACTION.
HURRRRAAAY!!
THE END

Grab these other Graphic Guide Adventures...

WILD RIDE
A GRAPHIC GUIDE ADVENTURE
LIAM O'DONNELL
MIKE DEAS

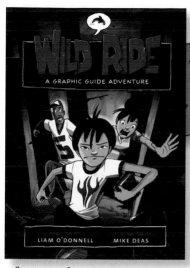

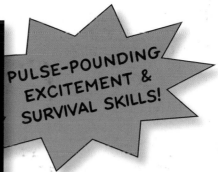

PULSE-POUNDING EXCITEMENT & SURVIVAL SKILLS!

AFTER THEIR PLANE GOES DOWN IN RUGGED WILDERNESS, DEVIN, NADIA AND MARCUS STRUGGLE TO SURVIVE. ADVENTURE, DANGER AND SURVIVAL SKILLS (AND BEARS. OH MY!)

978-1-55143-756-9

EXCITEMENT, ACTION & SOME RADICAL SKATING TIPS!

RAMP RATS
A GRAPHIC GUIDE ADVENTURE
WRITTEN BY
LIAM O'DONNELL
ILLUSTRATED BY
MIKE DEAS

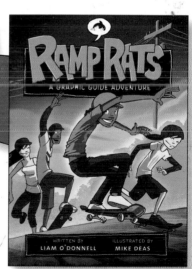

BETWEEN LEARNING HOW TO OLLIE AND DO A 50-50 GRIND, BOUNCE AND HIS FRIENDS HAVE TO AVOID THE SKATE-PARK GOONS AND TAKE ON A GANG OF OUTLAW BIKERS. A JUNIOR LIBRARY GUILD SELECTION.

978-1-55143-880-1

"Aside from the action-packed story, great characters, and colorful artwork, this graphic novel adventure includes an array of practical skateboarding tips for beginners."
—*Booklist*

And coming in fall 2009—Media Makers!

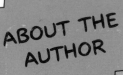

ABOUT THE AUTHOR

FROM CHAPTER BOOKS TO COMIC STRIPS, **LIAM O'DONNELL** WRITES FICTION AND NON-FICTION FOR YOUNG READERS. HE IS THE AUTHOR OF THE AWARD-WINNING SERIES "MAX FINDER MYSTERY." LIAM LIVES IN TORONTO, ONTARIO.

ABOUT THE ILLUSTRATOR

MIKE DEAS IS A TALENTED ILLUSTRATOR IN A NUMBER OF DIFFERENT GENRES. HE GRADUATED FROM CAPILANO COLLEGE'S COMMERCIAL ANIMATION PROGRAM AND HAS WORKED AS A GAME DEVELOPER. MIKE LIVES IN VICTORIA, BRITISH COLUMBIA.